The Kingdom of This World

By the same author:

The Kingdom
OF This World

BY *Alejo Carpentier*

TRANSLATED FROM THE SPANISH
BY HARRIET DE ONÍS

VICTOR GOLLANCZ LTD

LONDON

1967

Originally published in Spanish in 1949 as EL REINO DE ESTE
MUNDO *by* E. D. I. A. P. S. A. *in Mexico,* D. F.
The English version of lines from Racine's PHÈDRE *is quoted, by
permission of the Oxford University Press, from* THE BEST
PLAYS OF RACINE. *Translated by Lacy Lockert, copyright, 1936,
by Oxford University Press.*

Printed in Great Britain by
Lowe and Brydone (Printers) Ltd., London

Part One

Part Two

Part Three

Part Four

Part One

THE DEVIL
  Permission to enter I seek . . .

PROVIDENCE
  Who are you?

THE DEVIL
  The King of the West.

PROVIDENCE
  I know you, accursed one.
  Come in.

  (*He enters*)

THE DEVIL
  Oh, blessed court,
  Eternal Providence!
  Where are you sending Columbus
  To renew my evil deeds?
  Know you not that long since
  I rule there?

                              —Lope de Vega

I *The Wax Heads*

Of the twenty stallions brought to Cap Français by the ship's captain, who had a kind of partnership with a breeder in Normandy, Ti Noël had unhesitatingly picked that stud with the four white feet and rounded crupper which promised good service for mares whose colts were coming smaller each year. M. Lenormand de Mézy, who knew the slave's gift for judging horse flesh, had paid the price in ringing *louis d'or* without questioning his choice. Ti Noël had fashioned a headstall of rope, and had felt with satisfaction the breadth of the heavy dappled beast, sensing against his thighs the lather of sweat that gave an acid reek to the percheron's thick coat. Following his master, who was riding a lighter-limbed sorrel, he crossed the sailors' quarter with its shops smelling of brine, its sailcloth stiffened by the dampness, its hardtack that it took a fist-blow to break, coming out on the main street iridescent at that hour of the morning with the bright checked bandannas of the Negresses on their way home from market. From the carriage of the Governor, with its heavy gilded trim, a fulsome greeting floated to M. Lenormand de Mézy. Then squire and slave tied their horses before the shop of the barber who subscribed to the *Leyden Gazette* for the enlightenment of his educated customers.

While his master was being shaved, Ti Noël could gaze his fill at the four wax heads that adorned the counter by the door. The curls of the wigs, opening into a pool of ringlets on the red baize, framed expressionless faces. Those heads seemed as real—although their fixed stare was so dead—as the talking head an itinerant mountebank had brought to the Cap years before to promote the sale of an elixir for curing toothache and rheumatism. By an amusing coincidence, in the window of the tripe-shop next door there were calves' heads, skinned and each with a sprig of parsley across the tongue, which possessed the same waxy quality. They seemed asleep among the pickled oxtails, calf's-foot jelly, and pots of tripe *à la mode de Caen*. Only a wooden wall separated the two counters, and it amused Ti Noël to think that alongside the pale calves' heads, heads of white men were served on the same tablecloth. Just as fowl for a banquet are adorned with their feathers, so some experienced, macabre cook might have trimmed the heads with their best wigs. All that was lacking was a border of lettuce leaves or radishes cut in the shape of lilies. Moreover, the jars of gum arabic, the bottles of lavender water, the boxes of rice powder, close neighbors to the kettles of tripe and the platters of kidneys, completed, with this coincidence of flasks and cruets, that picture of an abominable feast.

The morning was rampant with heads, for next to the tripe-shop the bookseller had hung on a wire with clothespins the latest prints received from Paris. At least four of them displayed the face of the King of France in a border of suns, swords, and laurel. But there were many other bewigged heads, probably those of high court dignitaries. The warriors could be identified by their air of setting out for battle; the judges, by their menacing frowns; the wits, by their smiles, above two crossed pens at the head of verses that meant nothing to Ti Noël, for the slaves were unable to read. There were also colored engravings of a lighter nature showing fireworks to celebrate the capture of a city, dance scenes in which doctors brandished big syringes, a game of blindman's buff in a park,

youthful libertines burying their hands in the
bodices of serving-maids, or the never-failing
stratagem of the lover lying on the sward and
gazing upward in delight at the foreshortened in-
timacies of the lady swaying innocently in a swing.
But Ti Noël's attention was attracted at that moment by a copper engraving, the last of the series,
which differed from the others in subject and
treatment. It represented a kind of French admiral
or ambassador being received by a Negro framed
by feather fans and seated upon a throne adorned
with figures of monkeys and lizards.

"What kind of people are those?" he boldly in-
quired of the bookseller, who was lighting a long
clay pipe in the doorway of his shop.

"That is a king of your country."

This confirmation of what he had supposed was
hardly necessary, for the young slave recalled those
tales Macandal sing-songed in the sugar mill while
the oldest horse on the Lenormand de Mézy plantation turned the cylinders. With deliberately languid tone, the better to secure certain effects, the
Mandingue Negro would tell of things that had
happened in the great kingdoms of Popo, of Arada,
of the Nagos, or the Fulah. He spoke of the great

migrations of tribes, of age-long wars, of epic bat-
tles in which the animals had been allies of men.
He knew the story of Adonhueso, of the King
of Angola, of King Da, the incarnation of the
Serpent, which is the eternal beginning, never
ending, who took his pleasure mystically with a
queen who was the Rainbow, patroness of the Waters and of all Bringing Forth. But, above all, it
was with the tale of Kankan Muza that he achieved
the gift of tongues, the fierce Muza, founder of
the invincible empire of the Mandingues, whose
horses went adorned with silver coins and embroidered housings, their neighs louder than the clang
of iron, bearing the thunder on two drumheads
that hung from their necks. Moreover, those kings
rode with lances in hand at the head of their hordes,
and they were made invulnerable by the science of
the Preparers, and fell wounded only if in some
way they had offended the gods of Lightning or of
the Forge. They were kings, true kings, and not
those sovereigns wigged in false hair who played
at cup and ball and were gods only when they
strutted the stage of their court theaters, effemi-
nately pointing a leg in the measures of a rigadoon.
These white monarchs lent more ear to the sym-

phonies of violins and the whisper of gossip, the tittle-tattle of their mistresses and the warble of their stringed birds, than to the roar of cannon against the spur of the crescent moon. Although Ti Noël had little learning, he had been instructed in these truths by the deep wisdom of Macandal. In Africa the king was warrior, hunter, judge, and priest; his precious seed distended hundreds of bellies with a mighty strain of heroes. In France, in Spain, the king sent his generals to fight in his stead; he was incompetent to decide legal problems, he allowed himself to be scolded by any trumpery friar. And when it came to a question of virility, the best he could do was engender some puling prince who could not bring down a deer without the help of stalkers, and who, with unconscious irony, bore the name of as harmless and silly a fish as the dolphin. Whereas Back There there were princes as hard as anvils, and princes who were leopards, and princes who knew the language of the forest, and princes who ruled the four points of the compass, lords of the clouds, of the seed, of bronze, of fire.

Ti Noël heard the voice of his master, who emerged from the barber's with heavily powdered cheeks. His face now bore a startling resemblance to the four dull wax faces that stood in a row along the counter, smiling stupidly. On his way out M. Lenormand de Mézy bought a calf's head in the tripe-shop, which he handed over to the slave. Astride the stallion panting for green pastures, Ti Noël clasped that white, chill skull under his arm, thinking how much it probably resembled the bald head of his master hidden beneath his wig. The Negresses returning from market had been replaced by ladies coming from ten o'clock Mass. Many a quadroon, the light-of-love of some rich official, was followed by a maid of her own equivocal hue, carrying her palm-leaf fan, her prayerbook, and her gold-tasseled parasol. On a corner a group of strolling players was dancing. Farther on a sailor was offering for sale to the ladies a Brazilian monkey in Spanish dress. In the taverns bottles of wine, cooled in barrels filled with salt and damp sand, were being uncorked. Father Corneille, the curate of Limonade, had just arrived at the Cathedral riding his donkey-colored mule.

M. Lenormand de Mézy and his slave left the city by the road that skirted the seashore. A salvo rang out from the parapets of the fortress. *La*

Courageuse, of His Majesty's fleet, had been sighted, returning from the Île de la Tortue. Its gunwales returned the echoes of the blank shells. Old memories of his days as petty officer stirred in the master's breast, and he began to whistle a fife march. Ti Noël, in a kind of mental counterpoint, silently hummed a chanty that was very popular among the harbor coopers, heaping ignominy on the King of England. This he was sure of, even though the words were not in Creole. Moreover, he had little esteem for the King of England, or the King of France, or of Spain, who ruled the other half of the Island, and whose wives, according to Macandal, tinted their cheeks with oxblood and buried fœtuses in a convent whose cellars were filled with skeletons that had been rejected by the true heaven, which wanted nothing to do with those who died ignoring the true gods.

☙

II   *The Amputation*

☙

Ti Noël had seated himself on an upturned trough, letting the old horse circle the mill at a pace that habit had made mechanical. Macandal fed in sheaves of cane, pushing them head first between the iron rollers. With his bloodshot eyes, his powerful torso, his incredibly slender waist, the Mandingue exercised a strange fascination over Ti Noël. It was said that his deep, opaque voice made him irresistible to the Negro women. And his narrative arts, when, with terrible gestures, he played the part of the different personages, held the men spellbound, especially when he recalled his trip, years earlier, as a prisoner before he was sold to the slave-traders of Sierra Leone. As Ti Noël listened to him, he realized that Cap Français, with its belfries, its stone buildings, its Norman houses with their long-roofed balconies across the front, was a trumpery thing compared with the cities of Guinea. There, cupolas of red clay rose above great fortresses surrounded by battlements; the markets were famous beyond the limits of the deserts, as far as the nomad tribes. In those cities the workmen were skilled in working metals, forging swords that cut like razors and weighed no more than a wing in the hand of the user. Great rivers rising in the sky licked men's feet, and there was no need to bring salt from the Land of Salt. Wheat, sesame, and millet were stored in great depots, and trade was carried on from kingdom to kingdom, even in olive oil and wines from Andalusia. Under palm-frond covers slept the giant drums, the mothers of drums, with legs painted red and human faces. The rains were under the control of the wise men, and at the feasts of circumcision, when the youths danced with bloodstained legs, sonorous stones were thumped to produce a music like that of tamed cataracts. In the holy city of Whidah, the Cobra was worshipped, the mystical representation of the eternal wheel, as were the gods who ruled the vegetable kingdom and appeared, wet and gleaming, among the canebrakes that muted the banks of the salt lakes.

The horse, stumbling, dropped to its knees. There came a howl so piercing and so prolonged that it reached the neighboring plantations, frightening the pigeons. Macandal's left hand had been caught with the cane by the sudden tug of the rollers, which had dragged in his arm up to the shoulder. An eye of blood began to widen in the pan catching the juice. Grabbing a knife, Ti Noël cut the traces that fastened the horse to the shaft of the mill. Slaves from the tannery rushed over, following the master, as did the meat-smokers and cacao-bean-dryers. Now Macandal was pulling at his crushed arm, turning the rollers backward. With his right hand he was trying to move an elbow, a wrist that no longer obeyed him. He had a stupefied look, as though he was not taking in what had happened to him. They began to tie a rope tourniquet under his armpit to stop the bleeding. The master called for the whetstone to sharpen the machete to be used in the amputation.

⚑

III   *What the Hand Found*
⚑

Incapacitated for heavier work, Macandal was put in charge of pasturing the cattle. Before daybreak he drove them out of the stables, heading them toward the mountain whose shady slopes were thick with grass that held the dew until morning was high. As he watched the slow scattering of the herd grazing knee-deep in clover, he developed a keen interest in the existence of certain plants to which nobody else paid attention. Stretched out in the shade of a carob tree, resting on the elbow of his sound arm, he foraged with his only hand among the familiar grasses for those spurned growths to which he had given no thought before. To his surprise he discovered the secret life of strange species given to disguise, confusion, and camouflage, protectors of the little armored beings that avoid the pathways of the ants. His hand gathered anonymous seeds, sulphury capers, diminutive hot peppers; vines that wove nets among the stones; solitary bushes with furry leaves that sweated at night; sensitive plants that closed at the mere sound of the human voice; pods that burst at midday with the pop of a flea cracked under the nail; creepers that plaited themselves in slimy tangles far from the sun. One vine produced a rash, another made the head of anyone resting in its shade swell up. But now what interested Macandal most was the fungi. There were those which smelled of wood rot, of medicine bottles, of cellars, of sickness, pushing through the ground in the shape of ears, ox-tongues, wrinkled excrescences, covered with exudations, opening their striped parasols in damp recesses, the homes of toads that slept or watched with open eyelids. The Mandingue crumbled the flesh of a fungus between

his fingers, and his nose caught the whiff of poison.
He held out his hand to a cow; she sniffed and
drew back her head with frightened eyes, snorting.
Macandal picked more fungi of the same species,
putting them in an untanned leather pouch hanging from his neck.

On the pretext of bathing the horses, Ti Noël
would absent himself for hours from the Lenormand de Mézy plantation and join the one-armed
man. Then both would make their way to the
edge of the valley, where the terrain became broken and the skirts of the mountains were perfo-
rated by deep caves. They stopped at the house of
an old woman who lived alone, though visitors
came to her from far away. Several swords hung
on the walls among red flags with heavy shafts,
horseshoes, meteorites, and wire hooks that held
rusty spoons hung to form a cross to keep off
Baron Samedi, Baron Piquant, Baron La Croix, and
other Lords of the Graveyards. Macandal showed
Maman Loi the leaves, the plants, the fungi, the
herbs he carried in his pouch. She examined them
carefully, crushing and smelling some of them,
throwing others away. At times the talk was of
extraordinary animals that had had human off-

spring. And of men whom certain spells turned into animals. Women had been raped by huge felines, and at night, had substituted roars for words. Once Maman Loi fell strangely silent as she was reaching the climax of a tale. In response to some mysterious order she ran to the kitchen, sinking her arms in a pot full of boiling oil. Ti Noël observed that her face reflected an unruffled indifference, and—which was stranger—that when she took her arms from the oil they showed no sign of blister or burn, despite the horrible sputter of frying he had heard a moment before. As Macandal seemed to accept this with complete calm, Ti Noël did his best to hide his amazement. And the conversation went placidly on between the Mandingue and the witch, with long pauses while they gazed afar.

One day they caught in heat a dog of the packs of Lenormand de Mézy. While Ti Noël, sitting astride the animal, held its head by the ears, Macandal rubbed its muzzle with a stone that the juice of a fungus had colored a light yellow. The dog's muscles contracted, its body jerked in violent convulsions, and it rolled over on its back, legs stiff and teeth bared.

That afternoon as they returned to the plantation, Macandal stood for a long time looking at the mills, the coffee- and cacao-drying sheds, the indigo works, the forges, the cisterns, and the meat-smoking platforms.

"The time has come," he said.

The next day when they called him, he was not there. The master organized a hunt merely for the benefit of the Negro hordes, without putting much effort into it. A one-armed slave was a trifling thing. Besides, it was common knowledge that every Mandingue was a potential fugitive. Mandingue was a synonym for intractable, rebellious, a devil. For that reason slaves from that kingdom brought a very poor price on the market. They all dreamed of taking to the hills. Anyway, with so many plantations on all sides, the crippled one would not get very far. When he was brought back, he would be tortured in front of the others to teach them a lesson. A one-armed man was nothing but a one-armed man. It would have been foolish to run the risk of losing a couple of good mastiffs whom Macandal might have tried to silence with his machete.

IV *The Reckoning*

Ti Noël was deeply distressed by Macandal's disappearance. If Macandal had suggested that he run away with him, Ti Noël would joyfully have accepted the mission of serving the Mandingue. Now he felt that Macandal had thought him too poor a thing to give him a share in his plans. During the long nights when this idea tormented him, he would get out of the manger where he slept and, weeping, throw his arms around the neck of the Norman stallion, burying his face in the warm, clean-smelling mane. The disappearance of Macandal was also the disappearance of all that world evoked by his tales. With him had gone Kankan Muza, Adonhoueso, the royal kings, and the Rainbow of Whidah. Life had lost its savor, and Ti Noël found himself bored by the Sunday dances and by always living with his animals, whose ears and perineums he kept scrupulously free of ticks. Thus the entire rainy season went by.

Close by the stables, one day when the rivers had returned to their beds, Ti Noël came upon the old woman of the mountain. She brought him a message from Macandal. In response, just at the break of dawn, the lad made his way into a narrow-mouthed cave covered with stalactites that pointed toward a deeper opening where bats hung by their feet. The floor was covered with a thick layer of guano that held petrified objects and fossil fish-bones. Ti Noël noticed that several clay jugs standing in the center gave off a heavy, bitter smell in the damp gloom. Lizard skins were piled on fern leaves. A large flat stone and several smooth round stones had been used recently for grinding. On a log stripped of its bark by machete slashes lay an account book stolen from the plantation's book-keeper, its pages showing heavy signs drawn in charcoal. Ti Noël was reminded of the herbalists' shops in the Cap, with their big brass mortars, their prescription books on stands, their jars of nux vomica and asafetida, their bunches of althea root for aching gums. All that was lacking was a few scorpions in alcohol, attar of roses, and a tank of leeches.

Macandal was thin. His muscles now moved at bone level, molding his thorax in bold relief. But his face, on which the candlelight brought out olive reflections, revealed a calm happiness. Around his head he wore a scarlet bandanna adorned with strings of beads. What amazed Ti Noël was the revelation of the long, patient labor the Mandingue had carried out since the night of his escape. It seemed that he had visited the plantations of the Plaine one by one, establishing direct contact with all who worked on them. He knew, for example, that in the indigo works of Dondon he could count on Olain, the gardener, Romaine, the cook of the slave-quarters, and one-eyed Jean-Pierrot; as for the Lenormand de Mézy plantation, he had sent messages to the three Pongué brothers, the bow-legged Fulah, the new Congolese, and to Marinette, the mulatto who had slept in the master's bed until she had been sent back to the washtub on the arrival of a certain Mlle de la Martinière, who had been married to him by proxy in a convent at Le Havre before embarking for the colony. He had also got in touch with two Angolese from beyond Le Bonnet de l'Évêque, whose buttocks were zebra-striped with scars from the red-hot irons applied as punishment for stealing brandy. In letters legible only to himself, Macandal had entered in his register the name of the Bocor of Milot, and even of drovers who were useful for crossing the mountains and making contact with the people of Artibonite.

Ti Noël learned that day what the one-armed man wanted of him. The very next Sunday the master, returning from Mass, was informed that the two best milch-cows on the plantation—the white-tailed ones brought from Rouen—were dying amid their droppings, their muzzles dripping bile. Ti Noël explained to him that animals brought in from foreign parts often could not distinguish between good grass and certain plants that poisoned their blood.

🖃

V   *De Profundis*
🖃

The poison crawled across the Plaine du Nord, invading pastures and stables. Nobody knew how it found its way into the grass and alfalfa, got mixed in with the bales of hay, climbed into the mangers. The fact was that cows, oxen, steers, horses, and sheep were dying by the hundreds, filling the whole countryside with an ever-present stench of carrion. Great fires were kindled at night-fall, giving off a heavy, oily smoke before dying out among heaps of blackened skulls, charred ribs, hooves reddened by the flames. The most experienced herbalists of the Cap sought in vain for the leaf, the gum, the sap that might be carrying the plague. The beasts went on falling, their bellies distended, encircled by swarms of buzzing bottle-flies. The rooftrees were alive with great black bald birds awaiting the moment to drop and rip the hides, tense to bursting, with their beaks, releasing new putrefaction.

Soon, to the general horror, it became known that the poison had got into the houses. One evening, after his afternoon repast, the master of Coq-Chante plantation had suddenly dropped dead without any previous complaint, dragging down in his fall the clock he was winding. Before the news could reach the neighboring plantations, other owners had been struck down by the poison, which lurked, as though waiting to spring, in glasses on night tables, soup tureens, medicine bottles, in bread, wine, fruit, and salt. The sinister hammering of coffins could be heard at all hours. At every turn in the road a funeral procession was encountered. All that was heard in the churches of the Cap was the Office for the Dead, and the last rites always arrived too late, ushered in by distant bells tolling new deaths. The priests had had to shorten the service in order to be able to care for all the bereaved families. Throughout the Plaine the identical prayers for the dead echoed lugubriously, converted into a hymn of terror. For terror was gaunting the faces and choking the throats. In the shadow of the silver crucifixes that moved up and down the roads, green poison, yellow poison, or poison that had no color went creeping along, coming down the kitchen chimneys, slipping through the cracks of locked doors, like some irrepressible creeper seeking the shade to turn bodies to shades. From *Miserere* to *De Profundis* the voices of the subchanters went on, hour after hour, in a sinister antiphony.

Exasperated with fear, drunk with wine because they no longer dared taste the water of the wells, the colonists whipped and tortured their slaves, trying to find an explanation. But the poison went on decimating families and wiping out grownups and children. Nor could prayers, doctors, vows to saints, or the worthless incantations of a Breton sailor, a necromancer and healer, check the secret advance of death. With involuntary haste to occupy the last grave left in the cemetery, Mme Lenormand de Mézy died on Whitsunday a little while after tasting a particularly tempting orange that an over-obliging limb had put within her reach. A state of siege had been declared on the Plaine. Anyone walking through the fields or near the houses after sunset was shot down without warning. The garrison of the Cap had paraded the roads, ridiculously threatening an intangible enemy with dire death. But the poison continued to mount mouth-high by the most unexpected routes. One day the eight members of the Du Périgny family found it in a keg of cider that they had brought with their own hands from the hold of a ship that had just docked. Putrefaction had claimed the entire region for its own.

One afternoon when they threatened to let him have a load of buckshot in the ass, the bowlegged Fulah finally talked. Macandal, the one-armed, now a *houngan* of the Rada rite, invested with superhuman powers as the result of his possession by the major gods on several occasions, was the Lord of Poison. Endowed with supreme authority by the

Rulers of the Other Shore, he had proclaimed the crusade of extermination, chosen as he was to wipe out the whites and create a great empire of free Negroes in Santo Domingo. Thousands of slaves obeyed him blindly. Nobody could halt the march of the poison.

This revelation set off a whirlwind of whiplashes on the plantation. And when the buckshot, fired in pure rage, had blasted the bowels of the black informer, a messenger was sent off to the Cap. That very afternoon all available men were mobilized to track down Macandal. The Plaine—stinking with green flesh, charred hooves, the domain of the worms—echoed with barks and blasphemies.

🦅

VI *The Metamorphoses*

🦅

For several weeks the soldiers of the Cap garrison and the search parties made up of planters, bookkeepers, and overseers beat the neighborhood, tree by tree, gulch by gulch, canebrake by canebrake, without finding any trace of Macandal. Moreover, the poison, now that its source was known, had halted its attack, returning to the jars the armless man probably buried somewhere, bubbling in the dark night of the earth, which had become night of the earth for so many of the living. The dogs and men returned from the hills at nightfall, sweating fatigue and frustration from every pore. Now that death had resumed its normal rhythm, its tempo accelerated only by certain raw winds of January or fevers brought on by the rains, the planters gave themselves over to drinking and card-playing, demoralized by their forced association with the soldiery. Between indecent songs and sharpers' tricks and fondling the Negresses' breasts as they brought in clean glasses, they recounted the feats of grandfathers who had taken part in the sack of Cartagena or had lined their pockets with the treasures of the Spanish Crown when Piet Hein, Peg-Leg, had brought off the fabulous attempt freebooters had dreamed of for two hundred years. Over tables stained with wine, between tosses of dice, they proposed toasts to L'Esnambuc, to Bertrand d'Ogeron, Du Rausset, and those men with hairy chests who had founded the colony on their own initiative making their will law, without ever being intimidated by edicts issued in Paris or the gentle reprimands of the *Code Noir*. Asleep under the stools, the dogs enjoyed the freedom from their spiked collars.

With lazing around in siestas and guzzling in the shade of the trees, the search for Macandal had slowed down. Several months had elasped without word of him. Some thought he had taken refuge in the interior, among the cloudy heights of the Great Highlands, there where the Negroes danced fandangos to the rhythm of castanets. Others stated that the *houngan* had got away on a schooner, and was operating in the region of Jacmel, where many men who had died tilled the land as long as they were kept from tasting salt. Nevertheless, the slaves displayed a defiant good humor. Never had those whose task it was to set the rhythm for the corn-grinding or the cane-cutting thumped their drums more briskly. At night in their quarters and cabins the Negroes communicated to one another, with great rejoicing, the strangest news: a green lizard had warmed its back on the roof of the tobacco barn; someone had seen a night moth flying at noon; a big dog, with bristling hair, had dashed through the house, carrying off a haunch of venison; a gannet—so far from the sea!—had shaken the lice from its wings over the arbor of the back patio.

They all knew that the green lizard, the night moth, the strange dog, the incredible gannet, were nothing but disguises. As he had the power to take the shape of hoofed animal, bird, fish, or insect, Macandal continually visited the plantations of the Plaine to watch over his faithful and find out if they still had faith in his return. In one metamorphosis or another, the one-armed was everywhere, having recovered his corporeal integrity in animal guise. With wings one day, spurs another, galloping or crawling, he had made himself master of the courses of the underground streams, the caverns of the seacoast, and the treetops, and now ruled the whole island. His powers were boundless. He could as easily cover a mare as rest in the cool of a cistern, swing on the swaying branches of a *huisache*, or slip through a keyhole. The dogs did not bark at him; he changed his shadow at will. It was because of him that a Negress gave birth to a child with a wild boar's face. At night he appeared on the roads in the skin of a black goat with fire-tipped horns. One day he would give the sign for the great uprising, and the Lords of Back There, headed by Damballah, the Master of the Roads, and Ogoun, Master of the Swords, would bring the thunder and lightning and unleash the cyclone that would round out the work of men's hands. In that great hour—said Ti Noël—the blood of the whites would run into the brooks, and the Loas, drunk with joy, would bury their faces in it and drink until their lungs were full.

The anxious wait lasted four years, and the alert ears never despaired of hearing, at any moment, the voice of the great conch shell which would bellow through the hills to announce to all that Macandal had completed the cycle of his metamorphoses, and stood poised once more, sinewy and hard, with testicles like rocks, on his own human legs.

🖋

VII *Human Guise*

🖋

After reinstating Marinette, the laundress, in his bedchamber for a while, M. Lenormand de Mézy, with the parish priest of Limonade acting as go-between, had married again, a rich widow, lame and devout. As a result, when the first northers

of that December began to blow, the house servants, directed by the new mistress's cane, began to
arrange Provençal saints around a papier-mâché
grotto, still smelling of warm glue, which would
be illuminated under the porch eaves during the
Christmas holidays. Toussaint, the cabinetmaker,
had carved the Three Wise Men in wood, but they
were too big for the Nativity, and in the end were
not set up, mainly because of the terrible whites
of Balthasar's eyes, which had been painted with
special care, and gave the impression of emerging
from a night of ebony with the terrible reproach
of a drowned man. Ti Noël and the other slaves
of the household staff watched the progress of the
Nativity, bearing in mind that the days of gifts
and midnight Masses were approaching, and that
what with visitors and festivities the masters' discipline became somewhat relaxed, leaving it
not too hard to come by a roast pig's ear in the
kitchen, take a swig of wine from the spigot of
the cask, or slip by night into the quarters of the
newly purchased Angola women whom the master
was going to mate, with Christian ceremony, after
the holidays. But Ti Noël knew that this time he
would not be around when the candles were lighted

and the gold of the grotto reflected their gleam. He would be far away that night, at the festival organized at the Dufrené plantation, to celebrate with a glass of Spanish brandy per person the birth of the first male in the house of the master.

> *Roulé, roulé, Congoa roulé!*
> *Roulé, roulé, Congoa roulé!*
> *A fort ti fille ya dansé congo ya-ya-ró!*

For more than two hours the drums had been booming under the light of the torches, the women's shoulders kept moving rhythmically in a gesture as though washing clothes, when a momentary tremor shook the voices of the singers. Behind the Mother Drum rose the human figure of Macandal. The Mandingue Macandal. The man Macandal. The One-Armed. The Restored. The Transformed. None spoke to him, but his glance met that of all. And the glasses of brandy began to move from hand to hand toward his single hand, which had known a long thirst. Ti Noël saw him for the first time since his metamorphoses. Something of his sojourns in mysterious places seemed to cling to him, something of his successive attires of scales, bristles, fur. His chin had taken on a feline sharpness, and his eyes seemed to slant a little toward his temples, like those of certain birds whose appearance he had assumed. The women passed before him, and passed again, their bodies swaying to the rhythm of the dance. But the air was so fraught with questions that suddenly, without previous agreement, all the voices joined in a *yenvaló* solemnly howled above the drumbeats. After the wait of four years, the chant became the recital of boundless suffering:

> *Yenvaló moin Papa!*
> *Moin pas mangé q'm bambo*
> *Yenvaló, Papa, yenvaló moin!*
> *Ou vlai moin lavé chaudier,*
> *Yenvaló moin?*

"Will I have to go on washing the vats? Will I have to go on eating bamboos?" As though wrenched from their vitals, the questions trod one on the other, taking on, in chorus, the rending despair of peoples carried into captivity to build pyramids, towers, or endless walls. "Oh, father, my father, how long is the road! Oh, father, my father, how long the suffering!" With so much lamentation, Ti Noël had forgotten that the whites, too, have ears. For that reason, in the patio of the Dufrené big house at that very moment balls were being rammed into all the muskets, blunderbusses, and pistols that had been lifted down from their places on the wall. And, to provide for all contingencies, a supply of knives, rapiers, and clubs was left in the keeping of the women, who were already saying prayers and making rogations for the capture of the Mandingue.

🐦

VIII *The Great Flight*

🐦

One Monday in January, shortly before daybreak, the slaves of the plantations of the Plaine du Nord began to enter the city of the Cap. Shepherded by their masters and overseers on horseback, escorted by heavily armed guards, the slaves began to darken the city square while the military drums sounded a solemn beat. Several soldiers were piling faggots of wood at the foot of a *quebracho* post; others were adding fuel to a brazier. In the atrium of the principal church, alongside the Governor, the judges, and the Crown officials, the ecclesiastic hierarchy sat in tall red armchairs in the shade of a funeral canopy stretched upon rods and braces. Bright parasols moved in the balconies, like the gay nodding of flowers in a windowbox. As though talking from loge to loge in a huge theater, the women, fans in their mittened hands, chattered loudly, their voices delightfully excited. Those whose windows gave upon the square had prepared refreshments of lemonade and orgeat for their guests. Below, more tightly packed and sweaty every minute, the Negroes awaited the performance that had been prepared for them, a gala function for Negroes on whose splendor no expense had been spared. For this time the lesson was to be driven home with fire, not blood, and certain illuminations, lighted to be remembered, were very costly.

At a given moment all the fans snapped shut. There was a great silence behind the military drums. Macandal, his waist girded by striped pants, bound with ropes and knots, his skin gleaming with recent wounds, was moving toward the center of the square. The masters' eyes questioned the faces of the slaves. But the Negroes showed spiteful indifference. What did the whites know of Negro matters? In his cycle of metamorphoses, Macandal had often entered the mysterious world of the insects, making up for the lack of his human arm with the possession of several feet, four wings, or long antennæ. He had been fly, centipede, moth, ant, tarantula, ladybug, even a glow-worm with phosphorescent green lights. When the moment came, the bonds of the Mandingue, no longer possessing a body to bind, would trace the shape of a man in the air for a second before they slipped down the post. And Macandal, transformed into a buzzing mosquito, would light on the very tricorne of the commander of the troops to laugh at the dismay of the whites. This was what the masters did not know; for that reason they had squandered so much money putting on this useless show, which would prove how completely helpless they were against a man chrismed by the great Loas.

Macandal was now lashed to the post. The executioner had picked up an ember with the tongs. With a gesture rehearsed the evening before in front of a mirror, the Governor unsheathed his dress sword and gave the order for the sentence to be carried out. The fire began to rise toward the Mandingue, licking his legs. At that moment

Macandal moved the stump of his arm, which they had been unable to tie up, in a threatening gesture which was none the less terrible for being partial, howling unknown spells and violently thrusting his torso forward. The bonds fell off and the body of the Negro rose in the air, flying overhead, until it plunged into the black waves of the sea of slaves. A single cry filled the square:

"Macandal saved!"

Pandemonium followed. The guards fell with rifle butts on the howling blacks, who now seemed to overflow the streets, climbing toward the windows. And the noise and screaming and uproar were such that very few saw that Macandal, held by ten soldiers, had been thrust head first into the fire, and that a flame fed by his burning hair had drowned his last cry. When the slaves were restored to order, the fire was burning normally like any fire of good wood, and the breeze blowing from the sea was lifting the smoke toward the windows where more than one lady who had fainted had recovered consciousness. There was no longer anything more to see.

That afternoon the slaves returned to their plantations laughing all the way. Macandal had kept his word, remaining in the Kingdom of This World. Once more the whites had been outwitted by the Mighty Powers of the Other Shore. And while M. Lenormand de Mézy in his nightcap commented with his devout wife on the Negroes' lack of feelings at the torture of one of their own—drawing therefrom a number of philosophical considerations on the inequality of the human races which he planned to develop in a speech larded with Latin quotations—Ti Noël got one of the kitchen wenches with twins, taking her three times in a manger of the stables.

Part Two

" . . . je lui dis qu'elle serait reine là-bas; qu'elle irait en palanquin; qu'une esclave serait attentive au moindre de ses mouvements pour exécuter sa volonté; qu'elle se promènerait sous les orangers en fleur; que les serpents ne devraient lui faire qucune peur, attendu qu'il n'y en avait pas dans les Antilles; que les sauvages n'étaient plus à craindre; que ce n'était pas là que la broche était mise pour rôtir les gens; enfin j'achevais mon discours en lui disant qu'elle serait bien jolie mise en créole."

—*Madame d'Abrantès*

(" . . . I told her that she would be queen out there; that she would go about in a palanquin; that a slave would watch her smallest gesture in order to carry out her wishes; that she would stroll under orange-trees in bloom; that she need not fear snakes, for there are no snakes in the Antilles; that the savages are not to be feared; that people are not roasted on spits out there; at the end I rounded out my speech by telling her that she would be very pretty dressed as a Creole.")

I *The Daughter of Minos and Pasiphaë*

Not long after the death of M. Lenormand de Mézy's second wife, Ti Noël had to go to the Cap to pick up some harness that had been ordered from Paris for state occasions. During those years the city had made remarkable progress. Nearly all the houses were of two stories, with wide-eaved balconies and high ogival doors trimmed with polished bolts or hinges with clover-shaped heads. There were more tailors, hatters, feather-workers, hairdressers; there was a shop that sold violas and transverse flutes, as well as the music of *contredanses* and sonatas. The bookseller displayed the latest number of the *Gazette de Saint-Domingue*, printed on thin paper with a border of vignettes and spaced leads. And, as a further luxury, a theater for drama and opera had been opened in the rue Vandreuil. This prosperity was particularly good for the rue des Espagnols, where the most prosperous visitors took lodgings at the Auberge de la Couronne, which Henri Christophe, the master chef, had just bought from Mlle Monjean, its former mistress. The Negro's dishes were famous for the perfection of their seasoning when he was trying to please a guest newly arrived from Paris, or, in his *olla podrida*, for the abundance of ingredients when he was catering to the appetite of some hungry Spaniard who had come from the other side of the island in clothes so outmoded that they seemed those of the old buccaneers. Moreover, Henri Christophe, in his high white cap in the smoky kitchen, had a magic touch with turtle vol-au-vent or wood pigeons. And when he put his hand to the mixing bowl, the fragrance of his puff paste carried as far as the rue des Trois Visages.

Bereaved once more, M. Lenormand de Mézy, without the least respect for the memory of the dear departed, became an assiduous visitor to the Cap theater, where actresses from Paris sang Jean-Jacques Rousseau's arias or loftily declaimed tragic alexandrines, pausing between hemistichs to wipe the sweat from their brows. An anonymous libel in verse, excoriating the inconstancy of certain widowers, revealed to the world that a rich planter of the Plaine was finding nightly solace in the lush Flemish beauty of Mlle Floridor, a graceless interpreter of the role of confidante, whose name always appeared at the end of the cast, but who was

uniquely gifted in the phallic arts. At her persuasion
the master had departed for Paris unexpectedly
when the season ended, leaving the management of
the plantation in the hands of a relative. But something strange had happened to him. After a few
months, a growing longing for sun, for space, for
abundance, for command, for Negresses tumbled
alongside a canefield, made it plain to him that
this "return to France," to which he had looked
forward for so many years, was no longer the key
to happiness for him. After all his cursing of the
colony, after all his diatribes against its climate
and his contempt for the boorishness of the upstart
colonists, he returned to the plantation, bringing
with him the actress, whom the Paris managers had
refused to hire because of her lack of dramatic
ability. And so, on Sundays, two splendid carriages
with liveried postilions en route to church once
more adorned the Plaine. In Mlle Floridor's con-
veyance—the lady insisted on using her stage
name—ten mulatto girls squirmed about on the
back seat, twittering incessantly while their blue
petticoats fluttered in the wind.

Twenty years had gone by in all this. Ti Noël
had fathered twelve children by one of the cooks.

44

The plantation was more flourishing than ever, with its roads bordered with ipecac and its vines already yielding a tart wine. Nevertheless, with advancing age M. Lenormand de Mézy had become cranky and drank heavily. He suffered from a perpetual erotomania that kept him panting after adolescent slave girls, the smell of whose skin drove him out of his mind. He multiplied the corporal punishments meted out to the men, especially those guilty of fornication outside the marriage bed. Meanwhile the actress, faded and gnawed by malaria, avenged her artistic failure on the Negresses who bathed her and combed her hair, ordering them whipped on the slightest pretext. There were nights when she took to the bottle. It was not unusual on such occasions for her to order all the slaves to turn out, and under the full moon, between belches of malmsey, to declaim before her captive audience the great roles she had never been allowed to interpret. Wrapped in her confidante's veils, the timid player of bit parts attacked with quavering voice the familiar bravura passages:

*Mes crimes désormais ont comblé la mesure
Je respire à la fois l'inceste et l'imposture*

Mes homicides mains, promptes à me venger,
Dans le sang innocent brûlent de se plonger.

> (*My sins are heaped*
> *Already to overflowing. I am steeped*
> *At once in incest and hypocrisy.*
> *My murderous hands, hot for avenging me,*
> *Are fain to plunge themselves in guiltless*
> *blood.*)

Agape with amazement, at a loss to know what
it was all about, but gathering from certain words
that in Creole, too, referred to misdemeanors whose
punishment ranged from a thrashing to having one's
head chopped off, the Negroes came to the con-
clusion that the lady must have committed many
crimes in days gone by, and that she was probably
in the colony to get away from the police of Paris,
like so many of the prostitutes in the Cap, who
had unsettled accounts with the metropolis. The
word "crime" was similar in the island patois;
everybody knew what judges were called in
French; and, as for hell and red devils, they had
been vividly described by the second wife of M.
Lenormand de Mézy, a grim censor of all sins of
the flesh. Nothing that this woman, wearing a white

robe that was transparent in the torchlight, was confessing was of an edifying nature:

> *Minos, juge aux enfers tous les pâles humains.*
> *Ah, combien frémira son ombre épouvantée,*
> *Lorsqu'il verra sa fille à ses yeux présentée,*
> *Contrainte d'avouer tant de forfaits divers,*
> *Et des crimes peut-être inconnus aux enfers!*

> (*Minos, below, judges the souls of men.*
> *Ah, how his shade aghast will shudder when*
> *He sees his child is come before his eyes,*
> *Forced to avow so many infamies*
> *Diverse, and even deeds unknown to hell!*)

In the face of such immorality, the slaves of the Lenormand de Mézy plantation continued unshaken in their reverence for Macandal. Ti Noël passed on the tales of the Mandingue to his children, teaching them simple little songs he had made up in Macandal's honor while currying and brushing the horses. Besides, it was a good thing to keep green the memory of the One-Armed, for though far away on important duties, he would return to this land when he was least expected.

II *The Solemn Pact*

The claps of thunder were echoing like avalanches
over the rocky ridges of Morne Rouge and dying
slowly away in the depths of the ravines when the
delegates from the various plantations of the Plaine
du Nord, covered with mud to the waist, shivering under their soaking shirts, reached the heart of
Bois Caïman. To make matters worse, the August
rain, which fell warm or cold as the wind shifted,
had been coming down with increasing fury ever
since the slave curfew had sounded. His pants
clinging to his groin, Ti Noël tried to protect his
head with a burlap sack folded in the shape of a
hood. In spite of the darkness, there was no possibility that a spy might have sneaked into the gathering. The word had been passed around at the
last minute by men who could be trusted. Although the voices were kept low, the buzz of the
conversations filled the forest, mingled with the
pervading presence of the rain falling on the trembling leaves.

Suddenly a mighty voice arose in the midst of

the congress of shadows, a voice whose ability to pass without intermediate stages from a deep to a shrill register gave a strange emphasis to its words. There was much of invocation and much of spell in that speech filled with angry inflections and shouts. It was Bouckman, the Jamaican, who was talking. Although the thunder drowned out whole phrases, Ti Noël managed to grasp that something had happened in France, and that some very powerful gentlemen had declared that the Negroes should be given their freedom, but that the rich landowners of the Cap, who were all monarchist sons of bitches, had refused to obey them. At this point Bouckman let the rain fall on the trees for a few seconds, as though waiting for the lightning that jagged across the sea. Then, when the thunder had died away, he stated that a pact had been sealed between the initiated on this side of the water and the great Loas of Africa to begin the war when the auspices were favorable. And out of the applause that rose about him came this final admonition:

"The white men's God orders the crime. Our gods demand vengeance from us. They will guide our arms and give us help. Destroy the image of the white man's God who thirsts for our tears; let us listen to the cry of freedom within ourselves."

The delegates had forgotten the rain running down them from chin to belly, stiffening the leather of their belts. A howl went up out of the storm. Beside Bouckman a bony, long-limbed Negress was brandishing a ritual machete.

Faï Ogoun, Faï Ogoun, Faï Ogoun, O!
Damballah m'ap tiré canon,
Faï Ogoun, Faï Ogoun, Faï Ogoun, O!
Damballah m'ap tiré canon!

Ogoun of the Irons, Ogoun the Warrior, Ogoun of the Forges, Ogoun Marshal, Ogoun of the Lances, Ogoun-Chango, Ogoun-Kankanikan, Ogoun-Batala, Ogoun-Panama, Ogoun-Bakoulé were now invoked by the priestess of the Rada amid the shouting of the shadows:

Ogoun Badagri
Général Sanglant,
Saizi z'orage
Ou scell'orage
Ou fait Kataoun z'éclai!

The machete suddenly buried itself in the belly of a black pig, which spewed forth guts and lungs in three squeals. Then, called by the name of their masters, for they had no other, the delegates came forward one by one to smear their lips with the foaming blood of the pig, caught in a big wooden bowl. Then they dropped face downward on the wet ground. Ti Noël, like the others, swore always to obey Bouckman. The Jamaican then clasped in his arms Jean-François, Biassou, and Jeannot, who would not return to their plantations that night. The general staff of the insurrection had been named. The signal would be given eight days later. It was possible that aid would come from the Spanish colonists on the other side of the island, bitter enemies of the French. And in view of the fact that a proclamation had to be drawn up and nobody knew how to write, someone remembered the goose quill of the Abbé de la Haye, priest of Dondon, an admirer of Voltaire who had shown signs of unequivocal sympathy for the Negroes ever since he had read the Declaration of the Rights of Man.

As the rain had swollen the rivers, Ti Noël had to swim the slimy brook to be in the stable before the overseer woke up. The dawn bell found him sitting and singing, up to his waist in a pile of fresh esparto grass that smelled of the sun.

🐚

III   *The Call of the Conch Shells*
🐚

M. Lenormand de Mézy had been in a vile humor ever since his last visit to the Cap. Governor Blanchelande, a monarchist like himself, was completely out of patience with the vaporings of those Utopian imbeciles in Paris whose hearts bled for the black slaves. How easy it was to dream of the equality of men of all races between faro hands in the Café de la Régence or under the arcades of the Palais Royal. From views of the harbors of America decorated with compass cards and Tritons with wind-puffed cheeks; from pictures of indolent mulatto girls and naked washerwomen, of siestas under banana trees engraved by Abraham Brunias and exhibited in France along with verses of De Parny and the "Profession of Faith of the Savoyard Vicar," it was very easy to envisage Santo Domingo as the leafy paradise of *Paul and*

Virginia, where the melons did not hang from the branches of the trees only because they would would have killed the passers-by if they had fallen from such heights. In May, the Constituent Assembly, a mob of liberalists full of theories from the *Encyclopédie*, had voted to give the Negroes, sons of manumitted slaves, political rights. And now, faced with the specter of a civil war threatened by the plantation owners, these visionaries *à la Stanislaus de Wimpffen* answered: "Better the colonies should perish than a principle."

It must have been about ten at night when M. Lenormand de Mézy, weary of chewing the bitter cud of his reflections, went out to the tobacco shed with the idea of forcing one of the girls who slipped in at this hour to steal some leaves for their fathers to chew. From far off came the sound of a conch-shell trumpet. What was strange was that the slow bellow was answered by others in the hills and forests. And others floated in from farther off by the sea, from the direction of the farms of Milot. It was as though all the shell trumpets of the coast, all the Indian *lambis*, all the purple conchs that served as doorstops, all the shells that lay alone and petrified on the summits of the hills, had begun to sing in chorus. Suddenly, another conch raised its voice in the main quarters of the plantation. Others, higher-pitched, answered from the indigo works, from the tobacco shed, from the stable. M. Lenormand de Mézy, frightened, hid behind a clump of bougainvillaea.

All the doors of the quarters burst open at the same time, broken down from within. Armed with sticks, the slaves surrounded the houses of the overseers, seizing the tools. The bookkeeper, who had appeared, pistol in hand, was the first to fall, his throat slit from top to bottom by a mason's trowel. After bathing their arms in the blood of the white man, the Negroes ran toward the big house, shouting death to the master, to the Governor, to God, and to all the Frenchmen in the world. But, driven by a longstanding thirst, most of them rushed to the cellar looking for liquor. Pick-blows demolished kegs of salt fish. Their staves sprung, casks began to gush wine, reddening the women's skirts. Snatched up with shouts and shoves, the demijohns of brandy, the carboys of rum, were splintered against the walls. Laughing and scuffling, the Negroes went sliding through pickled tomatoes, capers, herring roe, and marjoram on the brick floor, a slime thinned by a stream of rancid oil flowing from a skin bag. A naked Negro, as a joke, jumped into a tub full of lard. Two old women were quarreling in Congolese over a clay pot. Hams and dried codfish tails were jerked from the ceiling. Sidestepping the mob, Ti Noël put his mouth to the bung of a barrel of Spanish wine and his Adam's apple rose and fell for a long time. Then followed by his older sons, he went up to the first floor of the house. For a long time now he had dreamed of raping Mlle Floridor. On those nights of tragic declamations she had displayed beneath the tunic with its Greek-key border breasts undamaged by the irreversible outrage of the years.

☙

IV *Dagon inside the Ark*
☙

After hiding for two days at the bottom of a dry well that was none the less gloomy for being shallow, M. Lenormand de Mézy, pale with hunger and fear, slowly raised his head above the wellcurb. All was silent. The horde had set out for the

Cap, leaving behind fires that had a name when one searched the base of the pillars of smoke that curved upward to the sky. A small powder magazine had just been blown up near Le Carrefour des Péres. The master approached the house, passing the swollen corpse of the bookkeeper. A horrible stench came from the burned kennels. There the Negroes had settled a long-pending score, smearing the doors with tar to make sure none of the dogs got through alive. M. Lenormand de Mézy directed his steps toward the bedroom. Mlle Floridor lay on the rug, legs sprawled wide, a sickle buried in her entrails. Her dead hand was still clenched around one of the bedposts in a gesture cruelly reminiscent of that of a sleeping girl in a licentious engraving entitled *The Dream* which adorned the wall. With groaning sobs, M. Lenormand de Mézy dropped beside her. Then he snatched up a rosary, and said all the prayers he knew, including one he had learned as a child to cure chilblains. Thus he spent several days, terrified, afraid to set foot outside the house given over, standing wide open, to its own ruin, until one day a messenger on horseback pulled up his mount so short in the back patio that it went head first against a window, striking sparks from the stones. His news, bellowed out, aroused M. Lenormand de Mézy from his stupor. The horde had been defeated. The head of the Jamaican, Bouckman, green and open-mouthed, was already crawling with worms on the very spot where Macandal's flesh had become stinking ashes. Total extermination of the Negroes was the order, but some armed groups were still sacking outlying dwellings. Without taking time to bury his wife, M. Lenormand de Mézy jumped up behind the messenger, who set out at a gallop on the road to the Cap. A burst of gunfire came from the distance. The messenger dug his heels into the horse's sides.

The master arrived in time to keep Ti Noël and a dozen other slaves bearing his brand from having their heads chopped off in the courtyard of the barracks. There the Negroes, tied back to back two by two, were being executed with machetes to save powder. These were the only slaves he had left, and the lot of them would bring at least six thousand five hundred Spanish pesos on the Havana market. M. Lenormand de Mézy urged that they be given the severest corporal punishment, but begged that the execution be put off until he had had a chance to talk with the Governor. Trembling with nervousness, insomnia, and too much coffee, M. Blancheland paced his office, adorned with a picture of Louis XVI, Marie-Antoinette, and the Dauphin. It was hard to make sense of his disordered monologue, in which vituperations of the philosophers alternated with quotations of prophetic warnings he had sent to Paris, to which he had not even received an answer. Anarchy was conquering the world. The colony faced ruin. The Negroes had violated nearly all the well-born girls of the Plaine. After ripping away so much lace, after rolling among so many linen sheets and cutting the throats of so many overseers, they could no longer be held down. M. Blancheland was in favor of the complete, absolute extermination of the slaves, as well as of the free Negroes and mulattoes. Anyone with African blood in his veins, quadroon, octoroon, sacatra, griffe—whatever the degree—should be put to death. It was foolish to be taken in by the cries of admiration the slaves uttered when the candles of the Nativity were lighted at Christmas-time. Father Labat had known what he was talking

about after his first visit to the island: the Negroes
were like the Philistines, adoring Dagon inside the
Ark. The Governor then pronounced a word to
which M. Lenormand de Mézy had not given the
least thought up to that moment: Voodoo. Now
he recalled how, years earlier, that ruddy, pleas-
ure-loving lawyer of the Cap, Moreau de Saint-
Méry, had collected considerable information on
the savage practices of the witch doctors in the
hills, bringing out the fact that some of the Negroes were snake-worshippers. Now that he remembered this, it filled him with uneasiness, making him realize that, in certain cases, a drum might
be more than just a goatskin stretched across a hollow log. The slaves evidently had a secret religion
that upheld and united them in their revolts. Pos-
sibly they had been carrying on the rites of this
religion under his very nose for years and years,
talking with one another on the festival drums
without his suspecting a thing. But could a civi-
lized person have been expected to concern himself with the savage beliefs of people who worshipped a snake?

Greatly depressed by the Governor's pessimism,
M. Lenormand de Mézy wandered aimlessly

through the city streets until nightfall. He feasted his eyes on Bouckman's head, spitting insults at it until he got tired of repeating the same obscenities. He spent a while at the house of the fat Louison woman, whose girls, in tight-fitting white muslin, fanned their bare breasts in a patio full of potted caladiums. But everywhere the atmosphere was disagreeable. So he set out for the rue des Espagnols to have a drink at the Auberge de la Couronne. When he saw the closed doors, he recalled that the cook, Henri Christophe, had given up the business for the uniform of the colonial artillery shortly before. Since the tin crown had been taken down, which for so long had been the sign of the inn, a gentleman could not eat decently in the Cap. His spirits raised a little by a glass of rum he drank over a counter, M. Lenormand de Mézy made arrangements with the owner of a coal-hooker which had been laid up for repairs for months, and which would be setting out for Santiago de Cuba as soon as it was caulked.

V *Santiago de Cuba*

The hooker had rounded the cape of the Cap. Behind, the city lay under constant menace from the Negroes, who knew they could count on arms offered by the Spaniards and on the fervor with which certain humanitarian Jacobins were beginning to defend their cause. While Ti Noël and his companions lay sweating in the hold on bags of coal, the first-class passengers, gathered in the poop, took deep breaths of the mild breezes blowing off the Strait of the Winds. There was a singer from the new company at the Cap whose hotel had been burned down the night of the uprising, and whose only dress was the costume of Dido the Forsaken; an Alsatian musician who had managed to save his clavichord, which the salt air had put out of tune, who occasionally broke off a measure of one of Johann Friedrich Edelmann's sonatas to watch a flying fish leap over a bank of yellow clams. A monarchist marquis, two republican officers, a lacemaker, and an Italian priest carrying the monstrance of his church completed the passenger list.

The night of their arrival in Santiago, M. Lenormand de Mézy made straight for the Tívoli, the palm-thatched theater recently erected by the first French refugees, for the Cuban inns with their flyswatters and hired donkeys at the entrance disgusted him. After so much anxiety, so much fear, such changes, he found the atmosphere of that *café chantant* comforting. The best tables were occupied by old friends of his, landowners who, like himself, had fled from the machetes whetted with molasses. But the strange thing was that with their fortunes gone, ruined, half their families unaccounted for, and their daughters convalescing from the Negro rapings—which was no small thing—the old colonists, far from bemoaning their situation, seemed to have taken a new lease on life. While others more foresighted than they had got their money out of Santo Domingo and had gone to New Orleans, or were starting new coffee plantations in Cuba, those who had salvaged nothing reveled in their improvidence, in living from day to day, in freedom from obligations, seeking, for the moment, to suck from everything what pleasure they could find. The widower discovered the advantages of being single; the respectable wife gave herself over to adultery with the enthusiasm of an inventor; the soldiers rejoiced in the absence of reveilles; young Protestant ladies came to know the flattery of the boards, appearing before the public in make-up and beauty spots. All the bourgeois norms had come tumbling down. What mattered now was to play the trumpet, give a brilliant performance in a minuet trio, or even strike the triangle on the right beat for the greater glory of the Tívoli orchestra. Sometime notaries now copied music; former tax-collectors painted twenty Solomonic columns on twelve-foot curtains. At rehearsal-time, when all Santiago was taking a siesta behind wooden shutters and nail-studded doors alongside monstrous dusty images from the preceding Corpus Christi Day, it was not unusual to hear some matron, once famed for her piety, singing with languid intonations:

Sous ses lois l'amour veut qu'on jouisse
D'un bonheur qui jamais ne finisse! . . .

*(Love, by its laws, desires us to enjoy
A happiness that never ends.)*

A great pastoral ball—a fashion now outmoded
in Paris—was being planned, and for its costum-
ing all the trunks salvaged from Negro rapine
were being pooled. The palm-frond dressing-
rooms were scenes of pleasant encounters while
some baritone husband, carried away by his role,
was immobilized on the stage by the bravura aria
of Monsigny's *Le Déserteur.* For the first time
Santiago de Cuba heard the music of *passepieds* and
contredanses. The last powdered wigs of the cen-
tury, worn by the daughters of the colonists,
swayed in time to the music of swift minuets that
were forerunners of the waltz. An air of license,
of fantasy, of disorder swept the city. The young
Cubans began to copy the fashions of the émigrés,
leaving to the members of the city council the always outdated Spanish attire. Unbeknownst to
their confessors, Cuban ladies took lessons in
French etiquette and practiced the art of turning
out their feet to show off the elegance of their
slippers. At night, when M. Lenormand de Mézy

attended the performance with a goodly number of drinks under his belt, he got to his feet with the rest, after the last number, to sing, in keeping with a custom established by the refugees themselves, the *Hymn of St. Louis* and the *Marseillaise*.

Lazy, unable to put his mind to any business venture, M. Lenormand de Mézy began to divide his hours between the card table and prayer. He sold off his slaves one by one to gamble away the money at cardhouses, pay his account at the Tívoli, or take home with him Negresses whose beat was the waterfront and who wore tuberoses in their kinky hair. But, at the same time, seeing in the mirror how the marks of age deepened with every passing week, he began to fear the approaching summons of God. Once a Mason, he now began to distrust the triangle. And so, accompanied by Ti Noël, he took to spending long hours groaning and rasping out ejaculatories in the Santiago Cathedral. While this went on, the Negro drowsed under the portrait of some bishop or watched the rehearsal of a Christmas cantata directed by a dried-up, loud-voiced, swarthy old man called Don Esteban Salas. It was really impossible to understand why this choirmaster, whom everyone

seemed to respect notwithstanding, was deter-
mined that the singers should enter the chorus one
after the other, part of them singing what the
others had sung before, and setting up a confusion
of voices fit to exasperate anyone. But this was undoubtedly pleasing to the verger, a personage to
whom Ti Noël attributed great ecclesiastical authority because he went armed and wore pants like
other men. Despite these discordant symphonies,
which Don Esteban Salas enriched with bassoons,
horns, and boy sopranos, the Negro found in the
Spanish churches a Voodoo warmth he had never
encountered in the Sulpician churches of the Cap.
The baroque golds, the human hair of the Christs,
the mystery of the richly carved confessionals, the
guardian dog of the Dominicans, the dragons
crushed under saintly feet, the pig of St. Anthony,
the dubious color of St. Benedict, the black Vir-
gins, the St. Georges with the buskins and corselets
of actors in French tragedies, the shepherds' instruments played on Christmas Eve had an attrac-
tion, a power of seduction in presence, symbols,
attributes, and signs similar to those of the altars
of the *houmforts* consecrated to Damballah, the
Snake god. Besides, St. James is Ogoun Faï,

c*

marshal of the storms, under whose spell Bouckman's followers had risen. For that reason Ti Noël,
by way of prayer, often chanted to him an old
song he had learned from Macandal:

> *Santiago, I am the son of war:*
> *Santiago,*
> *Can't you see I am the son of war?*

🦋

VI *The Ship of Dogs*
🦋

One morning the harbor of Santiago was filled
with barking. Chained to each other, growling and
slavering behind their muzzles, trying to bite their
keepers and one another, hurling themselves at the
people watching behind the grilled windows, hundreds of dogs were being driven with whips into
the hold of a sailing ship. More dogs arrived, and
still more, shepherded by plantation overseers, farm-
ers, and hunters in high boots. Ti Noël, who had
just bought a porgy for his master, approached the
strange ship into which they were still driving
dozens of mastiffs, which a French official was

counting with rapid clicks of the beads of an abacus.

"Where are they taking them?" Ti Noël shouted above the din to a mulatto sailor who was unfolding a net to stretch across a hatchway.

"To eat niggers!" the other answered with a guffaw.

This reply in Creole was a complete revelation to Ti Noël. He set out at a trot up the street toward the Cathedral, where he had become used to gathering with other French Negroes waiting for their masters to come out of Mass. The Dufrené family, having lost all hope of keeping their lands, had reached Santiago three days before, abandoning the plantation that had become famous by reason of Macandal's capture. The Dufrené Negroes had brought great news from the Cap.

From the minute she stepped on board, Pauline had felt a little like a queen on that frigate loaded with troops bound for the Antilles, its rigging creaking in time to the heaving of the broad, furrowed waves. From hearing her lover, the actor Lafont, declaim for her entertainment the most regal verses of *Bajazet* and *Mithridate*, she had be-

come familiar with queenly roles. Never over-
gifted with memory, Pauline vaguely recalled
something like "the Hellespont whitening beneath
our oars," which fitted in nicely with the wake of
foam which, *L'Océan*, its sails set, its pennants
fluttering, was leaving behind. But now each
change of wind carried off several alexandrines.
After having held up the departure of a whole
army because of a childish whim to make the trip
from Paris to Brest in a litter, she now had to put
her mind to more important things. Sealed hampers
carried kerchiefs brought from the island of Mau-
ritius, shepherdesses' basques, skirts of striped muslin that she planned to wear the first warm day,
having been briefed in all such matters by the
Duchess of Abrantès. After all, the trip was not
turning out too much of a bore. At the first Mass
said by the chaplain in the forecastle when they
had emerged from the rough waters of the Bay of
Biscay, all the officers had turned out in dress uniform, led by General Leclerc, her husband. There
were handsome specimens among them, and Pauline who, despite her tender years, was a connois-
seur of male flesh, felt delightfully flattered by the
mounting desire hidden behind the bowings and

scrapings and solicitude of which she was the object. She knew that when the lanterns rocked on the masts in the ever more brilliantly starred nights, hundreds of men were dreaming of her in staterooms, forecastle, and hold. For that reason she was so given to feigned meditations each morning, standing alongside the foresail, letting the wind ruffle her hair and play with her clothes, revealing the superb grace of her breasts.

A few days after sailing through the Azores Channel and contemplating in the distance the white chapels of the Portuguese villages, Pauline noticed that the sea was taking on new life. It was garlanded with what seemed to be clusters of yellow grapes drifting eastward, needlefish like green glass, jellyfish that looked like blue bladders, dragging after them long red filaments, repulsive, toothed garfish, and squids that seemed entangled in the transparencies of bridal veils. The brilliant officers began to unfasten their coats, following the example set by Leclerc, revealing shirt bosoms under open uniforms. One particularly sweltering night Pauline left her stateroom in her nightgown, and stretched out on the quarterdeck, where she had been in the habit of taking long afternoon naps.

The sea glowed green with strange phosphorescence. A slight coolness seemed to descend from the stars, which grew larger with every day's run. At dawn the lookout discovered, with pleasant surprise, a naked woman asleep on a folded sail in the shadow of the mizzenmast jib. Thinking her one of the stewardesses, he was on the point of sliding down a rope to join her. But a gesture of the sleeper, indicating that she was awakening, revealed to him that the body he was feasting his eyes on was that of Pauline Bonaparte. She rubbed her eyes, laughing like a child, her hair all blown about by the morning breeze, and, thinking herself protected by the canvas that hid the rest of the deck from her, poured several buckets of fresh water over her shoulders. From that night on she slept in the open, and her generous nonchalance became so well known that even wooden M. d'Esmenard, who was going out to organize the repression of the uprising, found himself dreaming with open eyes before the statue that was her body, evoking in her honor the Galatea of the Greeks.

The sight of the Cap and the Plaine du Nord, with the background of mountains blurred by the mist rising from the canefields, delighted Pauline, who had read *Paul and Virginia*, and had heard *L'Insulaire*, a charming Creole *contredanse* of exotic rhythm published in Paris on the rue du Saumon. Feeling herself part bird of paradise, part lyrebird, in her billowing muslin skirts, she discovered the delicacy of tender ferns, the brown juiciness of the medlar, leaves whose size made it possible to fold them like fans. At night Leclerc talked with furrowed brow of slave risings, of difficulties with the monarchist planters, of menaces of every sort. Fearing even greater dangers, he had arranged for the purchase of a house on the Île de la Tortue. But Pauline did not take him too seriously. She was still much moved by the reading of *Un Nègre comme il y a peu des blancs*, the lachrymose novel of Joseph Lavallée, and was enjoying to the full the luxury, the abundance that surrounded her, unlike anything she had known during a childhood in which dried figs, goat cheese, and rancid olives had been all too common. She lived not far from the principal church in a huge mansion of white stone surrounded by a shady garden. Under spreading tamarind trees she had ordered a swimming pool dug and lined with blue mosaic. There she bathed naked. At first she had herself massaged by her French maids; but one day it occurred to her that a man's hand would be stronger and more stimulating, and she engaged the services of Soliman, former attendant of a bath-house, who, besides caring for her body, rubbed her with almond cream, depilated her, and polished her toenails. While he was bathing her, Pauline took a perverse pleasure in grazing his flanks with her body under the water, for she knew that he was continually tortured by desire, and that he was always watching her out of the tail of his eye with the false meekness of a dog well-lessoned by the lash. She used to whip him with a green switch without hurting him, for the fun of seeing the faces of feigned suffering he made. As a matter of fact, she was grateful to him for the loving care he lavished on her beauty. For this reason at times she permitted the Negro, in return for an errand quickly carried out or a devoutly made communion, to kneel before her and kiss her feet in a gesture that Bernardin de Saint-Pierre would have interpreted as a symbol of the noble gratitude of a simple soul brought into contact with the generous teachings of the Enlightenment.

Thus she spent her time between siestas and waking, feeling herself part Virginia, part Atala, in spite of the fact that at times, when Leclerc was off in the south, she consoled herself with the youthful ardor of some handsome officer. But one afternoon the French coiffeur who was dressing her hair with the aid of four Negro assistants collapsed, vomiting up nauseous, half-clotted blood. A terrible killjoy in silver-spotted basque had come to disturb Pauline Bonaparte's tropical dream with its buzzing.

🦋

VII *Saint Calamity*
🦋

The next morning, at the insistence of Leclerc, who had just come through villages decimated by the plague, Pauline fled to La Tortue, accompanied by the Negro Soliman and maids loaded with bundles. She whiled away the first days bathing in a sandy cove and leafing through the memoirs of the surgeon Alexander Olivier Esquemeling, with its first-hand store of information on the habits and rascalities of the corsairs and buccaneers of America, who had left the ruins of an ugly fortress as a souvenir of their turbulent life on the island. She laughed when her bedroom mirror revealed to her that her skin, tanned by the sun, had become that of a splendid mulatto. But this interlude was of brief duration. One afternoon Leclerc landed on La Tortue, his body shaken by ominous chills. His eyes were yellow. The military doctor who accompanied him administered strong doses of rhubarb.

Pauline was terrified. To her mind came blurred memories of an epidemic of cholera in Ajaccio: black coffins carried out of the houses on the shoulders of men in black; widows in black veils who ululated at the foot of the fig trees; daughters garbed in black who attempted to throw themselves into their parents' graves and had to be dragged from the cemetery. She suddenly had one of those attacks of claustrophobia which she had so often suffered as a child. La Tortue, with its parched earth, its reddish cliffs, its wastes of cactus and locusts, its ever-present sea, seemed now her native island. Flight was impossible. Behind the door wheezed a man who had been so inconsiderate as to bring in death hidden under his galloons.

Convinced that the doctors could do nothing,
Pauline gave ear to the advice of Soliman, who
prescribed fumigation with incense, indigo, and
lemon peel and prayers of extraordinary effective-
ness such as those to the Great Judge, St. George,
and St. Calamity. She had the doors of the house
scoured with aromatic plants and tobacco strip-
pings. She knelt at the foot of a crucifix of dark
wood with ostentatious and somewhat peasant de-
votion, shouting with the Negro at the end of each
prayer: *Malo, Presto, Pasto, Effacio, AMEN.*
Moreover, those conjures, and driving nails to
form a cross in the trunk of a lemon tree, stirred
up in her the lees of old Corsican blood, which
was more akin to the living cosmogony of the Negro than to the lies of the Directory, in whose dis-
belief she had grown up. Now she repented of
having so often made a mock of holy things to
follow the fashion of the day. Leclerc's agony,
heightening her fear, drove her still farther toward
the world of the powers called up by the spells of
Soliman, now become the real master of the island,
the only possible defender against the plague from
the other shore, the only doctor among the useless prescripters. To prevent the evil miasmas

from crossing the water, the Negro set afloat little boats made of halves of coconuts, all bedecked with ribbons from Pauline's sewing box, which were in the nature of tributes to Aguasou, Lord of the Sea. One morning Pauline discovered a model of a man-of-war in Leclerc's luggage. She went running with it to the beach so Soliman might add this work of art to his offerings. Every means of defense had to be employed against the sickness: vows, penitence, hair shirts, fasts, invocations to whoever would lend an ear, even though at times it was the hairy ear of the Lying Enemy of her childhood. Suddenly, Pauline began to walk about the house in a strange manner, avoiding stepping on the cracks of the tiles, which—as everyone knew—were laid in squares at the impious instigation of the Masons, who wanted people to tread on the cross all day long. It was no longer scented perfumes, cool mint water that Soliman poured over her breast, but salves of brandy, crushed seeds, oily juices, and the blood of birds. One morning the horrified French maids came upon the Negro circling in a strange dance around Pauline, who was kneeling on the floor with her hair hanging loose. Soliman, wearing only a belt from which a white handkerchief hung as a *cache-sexe*, his neck adorned with blue and red beads, was hopping about like a bird and brandishing a rusty machete. Both were uttering deep groans which, as though wrenched from inside, sounded like the baying of dogs when the moon is full. A decapitated rooster was still fluttering amid scattered grains of corn. When the Negro saw that one of the maids was watching the scene, he angrily kicked the door shut. That afternoon several saints' images were found hanging from the rafters head down. Soliman, who now never left Pauline's side, slept in her room on a red rug.

The death of Leclerc, cut down by yellow fever, brought Pauline to the verge of madness. Now the tropics seemed abominable, with the relentless buzzard waiting on the roof of the house in which someone was sweating out his agony. After she had her husband's body, in dress uniform, laid in a cedar coffin, Pauline embarked with all haste aboard the *Swiftsure*, thin, hollow-eyed, her breast covered with scapulars. But before long, as the east wind brought Paris ever nearer the prow and the salt air tarnished the rings of the coffin, the young widow began to shed her cilices.

And one afternoon as the white-capped sea made the deck boards creak, her mourning veils became entangled in the spurs of a young officer, the one in charge of looking after General Leclerc's remains. In the hamper that contained her crumpled Creole disguises traveled an amulet to Papa Legba, wrought by Soliman, which was destined to open the paths to Rome for Pauline Bonaparte.

The departure of Pauline marked the end of such common sense as still existed in the colony. Under the government of Rochambeau, the remaining landowners of the Plaine, all hope of recovering their former prosperity gone, gave themselves over without let or hindrance to a vast orgy. Nobody paid any attention to clocks, nor did dawn mark the end of night. The watchword was eat, drink, and be merry before catastrophe swallows up all pleasure. The Governor granted favors in exchange for women. The ladies of the Cap mocked the late Leclerc's pronouncement that "white women who had prostituted themselves to Negroes were to be sent back to France, whatever their rank." Many women became tribades, appearing at dances with mulatto girls whom they called their cocottes. The daughters of slaves were forced while still infants. This was the road leading straight to horror. On holidays Rochambeau began to throw Negroes to his dogs, and when the beasts hesitated to sink their teeth into a human body before the brilliant, finely clad spectators, the victim was pricked with a sword to make the tempting blood flow. On the assumption that this would keep the Negroes in their place, the Governor had sent to Cuba for hundreds of mastiffs: "They'll be puking niggers!"

The day the ship Ti Noël had seen rode into the Cap, it tied up alongside another schooner coming from Martinique with a cargo of poisonous snakes which the general planned to turn loose on the Plaine so they would bite the peasants who lived in outlying cabins and who gave aid to the runaway slaves in the hills. But these snakes, creatures of Damballah, were to die without laying eggs, disappearing together with the last colonists of the *ancien régime*. Now the Great Loas smiled upon the Negroes' arms. Victory went to those who had warrior gods to invoke. Ogoun Badagri guided the cold steel charges against the last redoubts of the Goddess Reason. And, as in all combats deserving of memory because someone had made the sun stand still or brought down walls with a trumpet blast, in those days there were men who covered the mouths of the enemy cannon with their bare breasts and men who had the power to deflect leaden bullets from their bodies. It was then that there appeared about the countryside Negro priests, untonsured and unordained, who were known as the Fathers of the Savanna. When it came to praying in Latin at the pallet of the dying, they were as learned as the French priests. But they made themselves better understood, for when they recited the Lord's Prayer or the Hail Mary, they gave the words accents and inflections that made them like other hymns everyone knew. At last certain matters of life and death were being taken care of in the family.

Part Three

> Everywhere one came upon royal crowns of gold, some of them so heavy that it was an effort to pick them up.
>
> —Karl Ritter
> (a witness of the sack of Sans Souci)

I *The Portents*

A Negro, old, but still steady on his bunioned, calloused feet, stepped off the schooner that had just tied up at Quai Saint-Marc. Far off to the north, a mountain ridge outlined a familiar landscape in blue hardly darker than that of the sky. Without loss of time, Ti Noël, a stout lignum vitæ staff in hand, set out from the city. It was a long time now since the day a Santiago plantation-owner had won him in a card game by calling M. Lenormand de Mézy's bet. The latter had died soon after in the most abject poverty. Under his Cuban owner, Ti Noël's existence had been much more bearable than under the French of the Plaine du Nord. Saving up his Christmas money year after year, he had finally managed to get together the price of his passage on a fishing smack, sleeping on deck. Although twice branded, Ti Noël was a free man. He had now set foot on a land where slavery had been abolished forever.

His first day's travel brought him to the banks of the Artibonite, where he spent the night under a tree. The next morning he set out again, follow-

ing a road that ran between wild grape vines and
bamboos. Men who were bathing horses called out
words he did not understand very well, but which
he answered in his own fashion, saying the first
thing that came into his head. Besides, Ti Noël
was never alone even when he was alone. He had
long since acquired the art of talking with chairs,
pots, a guitar, even a cow or his own shadow.
These people were gay. But around a turn in the
road, plants and trees seemed to have dried up, to
have become skeletons of plants and trees in earth
which was no longer red and glossy, but had taken
on the look of dust in a cellar. There were no
bright cemeteries with little tombs of white plaster
like classic temples the size of dog-houses. Here
the dead were buried by the side of the road on
a grim, silent plain invaded by cactus and brush.
At times an abandoned roof on four poles told
of the flight of its inhabitants from malignant miasmas. Everything that grew here had sharp edges,
thorns, briers, evil saps. The few men Ti Noël
encountered did not reply to his greeting, plod-
ding by with their eyes to the ground like their
dogs' muzzles. Suddenly the Negro pulled up
short, catching his breath. A hanged he-goat dan-

gled from a thorn-covered tree. The ground was covered with signs: three stones forming a half-circle, a broken twig in the shape of a pointed arch like a doorway. Farther on, several black chickens swung head down along a greasy branch. Finally, where the signs ended, a particularly evil tree stood, its trunk bristling with black thorns, surrounded by offerings. Among its roots were thrust twisted, gnarled branches as crutches for Legba, the Lord of the Roads.

Ti Noël fell to his knees and gave thanks to heaven for allowing him the joy of returning to the land of the Great Pacts. For he knew—and all the French Negroes of Santiago de Cuba knew—that Dessalines's victory was the result of a vast coalition entered into by Loco, Petro, Ogoun Ferraille, Brise-Pimba, Caplaou-Pimba, Marinette Bois-Chèche, and all the deities of powder and fire, a coalition marked by a series of seizures of a violence so fearful that certain men had been thrown into the air or dashed against the ground by the spells. Then the blood, the gunpowder, the wheat flour, and the powdered coffee had been kneaded together to make the leaven that would turn men's heads toward the ancestors, while the sacred drums throbbed and across a fire the swords of the initiate clashed. When the exaltation reached fever pitch, one who had become possessed leaped to the backs of two men who were neighing and all were joined in the pawing profile of a centaur descending at a gallop toward the sea which, beyond the night, far beyond many nights, lapped the shores of the world of Mighty Powers.

II Sans Souci

After several days' journeying, Ti Noël began to recognize certain places. The taste of the water told him that he had often bathed, but lower down, in that brook which went winding toward the coast. He passed close to the cave where Macandal in days gone by had brewed his poisons. With mounting impatience he descended the narrow valley of Dondon to come out on the Plaine du Nord. Then, following the seashore, he made for the old plantation of Lenormand de Mézy.

By the three ceibas that formed a triangle he knew that he had arrived. But nothing was left there, neither indigo works, nor drying sheds, nor barns, nor meat-curing platforms. All that remained of the house was a brick chimney once covered with ivy, which, lacking shade, had pined away in the sun; only a few flagstones buried in the mud told where the warehouses had stood; of the chapel, all that was left was the iron cock of the weathervane. Here and there stood fragments of wall which looked like the thick, broken letters of an alphabet. The pines, the grapevines, the European trees had disappeared, as had the garden where, in olden days, the asparagus had raised its pale stalks, and artichokes had hidden their hearts in thick leaves amid the scent of mint and rosemary. The plantation had turned into a wasteland crossed by a road. Ti Noël sat down on one of the cornerstones of the old mansion, now a stone like any other stone for those who did not remember. He was talking to the ants when a sudden noise made him turn his head. Riding up at a swift trot came several horsemen in shining uniforms, with blue dolmans trimmed with frogs and loops, braid-embroidered collars, thickly fringed galloons, trousers of braid-trimmed chamois, plumed shakos, and hussar's boots. Accustomed as he was to the simple Spanish colonial uniforms, Ti Noël suddenly discovered with amazement the pomp of Napoleonic fashion to which the men of his race had given a degree of splendor the Corsican's generals had never dreamed of. The officers went by him in the direction of Milot as though enveloped in a cloud of gold dust. The old man, fascinated by the spectacle, followed the track of their horses in the dust of the road.

When he emerged from a grove he had the impression that he had come out into a sumptuous pleasure garden. All the land around the village of Milot was tended like a garden, with geometrically aligned irrigation ditches and flowerbeds green with tender seedlings. Many people were working these fields under the vigilance of soldiers carrying whips who occasionally shied a stone at some laggard. "Prisoners," thought Ti Noël to himself, as he observed that the custodians were Negroes, but that the workers were too, which ran counter to certain notions he had picked up in Santiago de Cuba on the nights when he had been able to attend some festive gathering of the French Negroes. But the old man stood still in his tracks, awed by the most unexpected, most

overwhelming sight of his long existence. Against
a background of mountains violet-striped by deep
gorges, rose a rose-colored palace, a fortress with
ogival windows, rendered almost ethereal by the
high socle of its stone stairway. To one side stood
long-roofed sheds that were probably workshops,
barracks, stables. To the other stood a round building crowned by a cupola resting on white columns
where surpliced priests went in and out. As he
drew nearer, Ti Noël could make out terraces,
statues, arcades, gardens, pergolas, artificial brooks,
and boxwood mazes. At the foot of heavy columns, which supported a great sun of black wood,
two bronze lions stood guard. Across the main
esplanade white-uniformed officers busily came
and went, young captains in bicornes, reflecting
the glitter of the sun, sabers rattling on their thighs.
Through an open window came the sound of a
dance orchestra in full rehearsal. In the palace windows ladies were visible, wearing plumed head-
dresses, their full busts pushed up by the high
waistlines of their fashionable gowns. In a patio
two coachmen were polishing a huge gilded coach
covered with suns in bas-relief. As he passed before
the circular building from which the priests had

D

emerged, Ti Noël saw that it was a church hung with curtains, banners, and canopies, which housed an image of the Immaculate Conception.

But what surprised Ti Noël most was the discovery that this marvelous world, the like of which the French governors of the Cap had never known, was a world of Negroes. Because those handsome, firm-buttocked ladies circling in a dance around a fountain of Tritons were Negresses; those two white-hosed ministers descending the main stairway with leather dispatch cases under their arms were Negroes; Negro was the chef, with an ermine tail on his cap, who was receiving a deer borne on the shoulders of several villagers led by the master huntsman; those hussars curvetting about the riding ring were Negroes; that high steward, with a silver chain around his neck, watching, in the company of the royal falconer, the rehearsals of Negro actors in an outdoor theater, was a Negro; those footmen in white wigs, whose golden buttons were being inspected by a butler in green livery, were Negroes; and, finally, Negro, good and Negro, was that Immaculate Conception standing above the high alter of the chapel, smiling sweetly upon the Negro musicians who were practicing a *Salve*. Ti Noël realized that he was at Sans Souci, the favorite residence of King Henri Christophe, former cook of the rue des Espagnols, master of the Auberge de la Couronne, who now struck off money bearing his initials above the proud motto *God, my cause and my sword*.

A heavy blow landed across the old man's back. Before he could utter a protest, a guard was herding him, with kicks in the behind, toward one of the barracks. When he found himself locked in a cell, Ti Noël began to shout that he was personally acquainted with Henri Christophe, and he even believed he had heard that he had married Marie-Louise Coidavid, the niece of a free lace-maker who had often come to the plantation of Lenormand de Mézy. But nobody paid any attention to him. In the afternoon he was led with other prisoners to the foot of Le Bonnet de l'Évêque, where great piles of building materials lay. He was handed a brick.

"Take that up, and come back for another one."

"I'm too old."

A cudgel cracked on Ti Noël's skull. Without further objections he began to climb the steep mountain, joining a long procession of children, pregnant girls, women, and old men, each of whom carried a brick. The old man looked back toward Milot. In the afternoon light the palace looked rosier than before. Before a bust of Pauline Bonaparte which had once adorned her house at the Cap, the little Princesses, Athenaïs and Améthyste, dressed in guipure-trimmed satin, were playing battledore and shuttlecock. A little farther off, the Queen's chaplain—the one light face in the whole picture—was reading Plutarch's *Parallel Lives* to the Crown Prince under the satisfied gaze of Henri Christophe, who was strolling, followed by his ministers, through the Queen's gardens. In passing, his Majesty's hand reached out carelessly to pick a white rose that had just opened amid the boxwood clipped in the shape of a crown and phœnix at the foot of the marble allegories.

₩

III   *The Sacrifice of the Bulls*
₩

Above the summit of Le Bonnet de l'Évêque, dentelated with scaffoldings, rose that second mountain—a mountain on a mountain—which was the Citadel La Ferrière. A lush growth of red fungi was mounting the flanks of the main tower with the terse smoothness of brocade, having already covered the foundations and buttresses, and was spreading polyp profiles over the ocher walls. That mass of fired brick, towering above the clouds in proportions whose perspective challenged visual habits, was honeycombed with tunnels, passageways, secret corridors, and chimneys all heavy with shadows. Light, as of an aquarium, a glaucous green tinted by ferns already meeting in space, fell above a vaporous mist from the high loopholes and air vents. The stairways to hell connected three main batteries with the powder magazine, the artillerymen's chapel, the kitchens, cisterns, forges, foundry, dungeons. Every day in the middle of the parade square several bulls had their throats cut so that their blood could be added to the mortar to make the fortress impregnable. On the side facing the sea and overlooking the dizzying panorama of the Plaine, the workers were already stuccoing the rooms of the Royal Palace, the women's quarters, the dining- and billiard-rooms. To wagon axles mortised into the walls were attached the suspension bridges over which brick and stone were carried to the topmost terraces, stretching between inner and outer abysses that filled the stomachs of the builders with vertigo. Often a Negro disappeared into space, carrying with him a hod of mortar. Another immediately took his place, and nobody gave further thought to the one who had fallen. Hundreds of men worked in the bowels of that vast edifice, always under the vigilance of whip and gun, accomplishing feats previously seen only in the imagined architecture of Piranesi. Hoisted by ropes up the face of the mountain, the first cannon were arriving and being mounted on cedar gun-carriages in shadowy vaulted rooms whose loopholes overlooked all the passes and approaches of the country. There stood the *Scipio*, the *Hannibal*, the *Hamilcar*, satin smooth, of a bronze that was almost gold in hue, together with those that had been cast after '89, with the still unproved motto of *Liberté*, *Égalité*. There stood a Spanish cannon whose barrel bore the melancholy inscription *Fiel pero desdichado;* and several of larger bore and more ornate barrel, stamped with the seal of the Sun King insolently proclaiming his *Ultima Ratio Regum*.

When Ti Noël laid his brick down at the foot of a wall it was almost midnight. Nevertheless, construction was going on by the light of bonfires and torches. Along the way men were sleeping on great blocks of stone, on cannon, beside mules whose knees were calloused from falling as they toiled upward. Worn out with fatigue, the old man dropped into a ditch under the suspension bridge. A whiplash awakened him at dawn. Above, the bulls who were to have their throats cut at daybreak were bellowing. New scaffoldings had come into being with the passing of the cold clouds, and the entire mountain came alive with neighing, shouts, bugle calls, whip cracks, the squeaking of dew-swollen ropes. Ti Noël began the descent to Milot in search of another brick. On the way down he could see coming up the flanks of the mountain, by every path and byway, thick columns of women, children, and old men, each with a brick to be left at the foot of the fortress, which was rising like an ant-hill, thanks to those grains of fired clay borne to it unceasingly, from season to season, from year's end to year's end. Ti Noël soon learned that this had been going on for more than twelve years, and that the entire population of the

North had been drafted for this incredible task. Every protest had been silenced in blood. Walking, walking, up and down, down and up, the Negro began to think that the chamber-music orchestras of Sans Souci, the splendor of the uniforms, and the statues of naked white women soaking up the sun on their scrolled pedestals among the sculptured boxwood hedging the flowerbeds were all the product of a slavery as abominable as that he had known on the plantation of M. Lenormand de Mézy. Even worse, for there was a limitless affront in being beaten by a Negro as black as oneself, as thick-lipped and wooly headed, as flatnosed; as low-born; perhaps branded, too. It was as though, in the same family, the children were to beat the parents, the grandson the grandmother, the daughters-in-law the mother who cooked for them. Besides, in other days, the colonists—except when they had lost their heads—had been careful not to kill their slaves, for dead slaves were money out of their pockets. Whereas here the death of a slave was no drain on the public funds. As long as there were black women to bear their children—and there always had been and always would be—there would never be a dearth of workers to carry bricks to the summit of Le Bonnet de l'Évêque.

King Henri Christophe often went up to the Citadel, escorted by a squad of officers on horseback, to observe how the work was progressing. Heavy-set, powerful, with a barrel-shaped chest, flat-nosed, his chin half-hidden in the embroidered collar of his uniform, the monarch examined the batteries, forges, and workshops, his spurs clinking as he mounted the interminable stairways. From his Napoleonic bicorne stared the bird's-eye of a two-colored cockade. At times, with a mere wave of his crop, he ordered the death of some sluggard surprised in flagrant idleness, or the execution of workers hoisting a block of granite too slowly up a steep incline. His visits always ended by his having an armchair brought out to the upper terrace that overlooked the sea from beside an abyss that made even those most accustomed to the sight close their eyes. Then, with nothing that could cast a shadow or care upon him, high above all, standing on his own shadow, he measured the scope of his power. In the event of any attempt by France to retake the island, he, Henri Christophe, *God, my cause and my sword*, could hold out here, above the clouds, for as long as was necessary, with his whole

D*

court, his army, his chaplains, his musicians, his African pages, his jesters. Fifteen thousand men could live with him within those Cyclopean walls and lack for nothing. Once the drawbridge of the Single Gate had been pulled up, the Citadel La Ferrière would be the country, with its independence, its monarch, its treasury, and all its pomp. Because down below, the sufferings involved in its building forgotten, the Negroes of the Plaine would raise their eyes to the fortress, replete with corn, with gunpowder, iron, and gold, thinking that there, higher than the birds, there, where life below was the remote sound of bells and the crowing of the roosters, a king of their own race was waiting, close to heaven, which is the same everywhere, for the thud of the bronze hoofs of Ogoun's ten thousand horses. Not for nothing had those towers arisen, on the mighty bellowing of bulls, bleeding, their testicles toward the sun, at the hands of builders well aware of the deep significance of the sacrifice even though they had told the ignorant that this represented an advance in the technique of military engineering.

⚑

IV   *The Immured*
⚑

When the work on the Citadel was drawing to a
close and there was more need of artisans than of
carriers of bricks, discipline was relaxed a little.
Even though mortars and culverins were still being
transported to the lofty cliffs, many women were
permitted to return to their cobwebbed cooking-
pots. Among those who were allowed to leave because of their scant usefulness, Ti Noël managed
to slip away one morning without turning his
head back toward the fortress now clear of scaf-
folding on the flank of the Princesses' Battery. The
logs now being rolled up the slopes with crowbars
were to be used as flooring for the living quarters.
But none of this any longer interested Ti Noël,
whose one thought was to set himself up on the
former lands of Lenormand de Mézy, to which
he was now returning like the eel to the mud in
which it was spawned. Back on the manor, feeling
himself in a way the owner of that land whose
contours were meaningful only to him, he began
to clear away some of the ruins with the help

of his machete. Two acacia trees, as they fell, revealed a piece of wall. From under the leaves of a wild squash the blue tiles of the dining-room emerged. Covering the cracked hearth of the old kitchen with palm fronds, the Negro fixed himself a bedroom that he had to enter on hands and knees, filling it with armfuls of dry grass to rest his body, bruised by the blows it had received along the trails of Le Bonnet de l'Évêque.

There he found refuge from the winds of winter and the rains that followed, and watched summer come in. His belly was swollen from eating too much green fruit, too many watery mangoes, for he kept away from the roads as much as he could to avoid Henri Christophe's men, who might be looking for workers to build some new palace, perhaps that one of which there was talk on the banks of the Artibonite, and which had as many windows as there were days in the year. But as the months went by without new developments, Ti Noël, his belly full of starvation, set out for the Cap, keeping to the seashore by the almost effaced trail he had so often traveled in other days, following his master, when he came back to the plantation riding a horse whose teeth did not yet meet, one of those whose trot had the sound of rubbed Cordovan leather and whose neck still showed the wrinkles of colthood. The city is good. In the city a forked stick can always find things to slip into a knapsack. In a city there are always kindhearted prostitutes ready to give an old man alms; there are markets with music, trained animals, talking dolls, and cooks who find it amusing when, instead of talking of hunger, one points to the brandy bottle. Ti Noël felt that a great chill was settling in the marrow of his bones. And he sighed for those bottles of other days—those in the cellar of the big houses—square, of thick glass, filled with peel, herbs, berries, and watercress steeped in alcohol, which reflected subdued hues of the most delicate odor.

But Ti Noël found the whole city in a death watch. It was as though all the windows and doors of the houses, all the jalousies, all the louvers, were turned toward the corner of the Archbishop's Palace with an expectation so intense that it distorted the façades into human grimaces. The roofs stretched out their eaves, the corners peered sharply forward, the dampness painted only ears upon the walls. At the corner of the Palace, a square of new cement had just dried, blending with the mortar of the wall, but leaving a small opening. Out of this hole, black as a toothless mouth, burst from time to time howls so horrifying as to send a shudder through the entire population and make the children sob. When this happened, pregnant women held their bellies with their hands and some of the passers-by took to their heels without completing the sign of the cross. And the howls, the senseless screams, continued at the corner of the Archbishop's Palace until the throat, choked in blood, lacerated itself in curses, dark threats, prophecies, and imprecations. Then they turned into weeping, a weeping that came from the depths of the breast, with the whimpering of a child in the voice of an old man, which was even more unbearable than what had preceded it. Finally the tears became a wheezing in three tempos, which gradually died away with a long asthmatic cadence until it was mere breathing. And this was repeated day and night at the corner of the Palace. Nobody slept in the Cap. Nobody dared to pass through the adjacent streets. Inside the houses, prayers were said in low voices in the innermost rooms. Nor would anyone have ventured even to comment

on what was happening. For that Capuchin immured in the Archbishop's Palace, buried alive in
its oratory, was Corneille Breille, the Duke of
Anse, confessor of Henri Christophe. He had been
condemned to die there, at the foot of a newly
plastered wall, for the crime of having wanted to
go to France knowing all the secrets of the King,
all the secrets of the Citadel whose red towers had
already been struck by lightning several times. In
vain Queen Marie-Louise pleaded for him, clasping
her husband's boots. Henri Christophe, who had
just insulted St. Peter for having sent a new storm
against his fortress, was not being frightened by
ineffectual excommunication by a French Capuchin. And, to remove any lingering doubt, there
was a new favorite at Sans Souci, a Spanish chaplain with a long tile hat, as given to running about
bearing tales as to singing Mass in his fine bass
voice, who was known to all as Father Juan de
Dios. Tired of the chick-peas and dried beef across
the mountains, the sly friar found the Haitian court
to his liking, where the ladies plied him with gla-
céed fruits and wines of Portugal. It was rumored
that certain words of his, spoken, as though offhand,
before Henri Christophe one day when he was

teaching his hounds to jump at the name of the King of France, were the cause of Corneille Breille's terrible disgrace.

After a week of incarceration, the Capuchin's voice had become almost inaudible, fading away to a death-rattle rather sensed than heard. And then silence came at the corner of the Archbishop's Palace. The over-prolonged silence of a city that had ceased to believe in silence and which only a newborn infant dared to break with its whimper of ignorance, rerouting life toward its customary sonority of street-cries, greetings, gossip, and songs sung while hanging clothes out in the sun. This was the moment when Ti Noël managed to stuff a few things in his sack and cadge enough money from a drunken sailor for five glasses of brandy, which he tossed off one after the other. Staggering in the moonlight, he set out for home, vaguely recalling a song that in other days he had sung on his way back from the city. A song that was all insults to a king. That was the important thing: *to a king*. And in this way, unburdening himself of every insult he could think up to Henri Christophe, his crown, and his progeny, Ti Noël found the way back so short that when he stretched him-

self out on his straw pallet, he even asked himself
if he had really gone to the Cap.

🦋

V *Chronicle of August 15*
🦋

*Quasi palma exaltata sum in Cades, et quasi plan-
tatio rosæ in Jericho. Quasi oliva speciosa in cam-
pis, et quasi platanus exaltata sum juxta aquam in
plateis. Sicut cinnamonum et balsamum aromati-
zans odorem dedi: quasi myrrha electa dedi sua-
vitatem odoris.*

Without understanding the Latin intoned by
Juan de Dios González with baritone inflections
of unfailing effect, Queen Marie-Louise found that
morning a mysterious harmony among the smell
of incense, the fragrance of the orange trees in
the near-by patio, and certain words of the liturgy
of the day which referred to perfumes whose
names were inscribed on the porcelain jars of the
apothecary's shop of Sans Souci. Henri Christophe,
on the other hand, was unable to follow the service
with due attention, for his breast was oppressed
by an anxiety he could not account for. Against

the advice of all, he had ordered the Mass of the Assumption sung in the church of Limonade, whose delicately veined gray marble gave a delightful impression of coolness so that one perspired a little less under the tightly buttoned swallow-tailed coat and the weight of decorations. Yet the King felt himself surrounded by a hostile atmosphere. The populace that had hailed him on his arrival was sullen with evil intentions, recalling all too well, there in that fertile land, the crops lost because the men were working on the Citadel. In some remote house—he suspected—there was probably an image of him stuck full of pins or hung head down with a knife plunged in the region of the heart. From far off there came from time to time the beat of drums which he felt sure were not imploring a long life for him. But the Offertory was beginning:

Assumpta est Maria in cælum; gaudent Angeli, collaudantes benedicunt Dominum, alleluia!

Suddenly, Juan de Dios González began to shrink back toward the royal chairs, clumsily stumbling against the three marble steps. The Queen's rosary fell from her fingers. The King's hand reached for the hilt of his sword. Before the altar, facing the worshippers, another priest had arisen, as though conjured out of the air, with part of his shoulders and arms still imperfectly fleshed out. And while his face was taking on contour and expression, from his lipless, toothless mouth, as black as a rat-hole, a thundering voice emerged which filled the nave with the vibrations of an organ with all stops pulled out, making the stained-glass windows tremble in their lead frames:

Absolve Domine, animas omnium fidelium defunctorum ab omni vinculo delictorum. . . .

The name of Corneille Breille stuck in the throat of Henri Christophe, leaving him dumb. Because it was the immured Archbishop, whose death and decay were known to all, who stood there before the high altar in his vestments intoning the *Dies Iræ.* When, thundering like the roll of a kettledrum, there arose the words *Coget omnes ante thronus,* Juan de Dios Gonzáles fell moaning at the feet of the Queen. Henri Christophe, his eyes starting from his head, bore it until the *Rex tremendæ majestatis.* At that moment a thunderbolt that deafened only his ears struck the church tower, shivering all the bells at once. The precentors, the thuribles, the choristers' stand, the pulpit had been cast down. The King lay on the floor paralyzed, his eyes riveted on the roof beams. Now, with a great bound, the specter had seated himself on one of these beams, in the very line of Henri Christophe's vision, spreading wide arms and legs as though the better to display his bloodstained brocades. A rhythm was growing in the King's ears which might have been that of his own veins or that of the drums being beaten in the hills. Carried out of the church in the arms of his officers, the King was mumbling curses, threatening all the inhabitants of Limonade with death if a rooster so much as crowed. While he was receiving first aid from Marie-Louise and the Princesses, the terrified countryfolk began stuffing hens and roosters into baskets and lowering them into the darkness of deep wells so they would forget their cackling and defiance. A rain of thwacks sent the startled donkeys down the hillside. The horses were muzzled lest their neighing give rise to wrong interpretations.

And that afternoon the royal carriage drawn by six galloping horses drew up at the esplanade of honor of Sans Souci. With shirt open, the King was carried to his chambers. He dropped on the bed like a sack of chains. His eyes, more cornea than iris, revealed a fury that came from the depths of his soul at being unable to move arms or legs. The doctors began to rub his inert body with a mixture of brandy, gunpowder, and capsicum. Throughout the Palace the smell of medicines, infusions, salts, ointments pervaded the warm air of the salons overflowing with officials and courtiers. The Princesses Athenaïs and Améthyste were weeping on the bosom of their North American governess. The Queen, with little thought for etiquette, was squatting in a corner of the antechamber watching over the boiling of a root brew on a charcoal brazier whose flame, reflected on a Gobelin showing Venus beside Vulcan's forge which adorned the wall, gave a strange realism to the colors of the tapestry. Her Majesty called for a fan to quicken the slow-burning fire. There was an evil atmosphere about that twilight of shadows closing in too quickly. It was impossible to know whether the drums were really throbbing in the hills. But at moments a rhythm coming from the distant heights mingled strangely with the *Ave Maria* the women were saying in the Throne Room,

arousing unacknowledged resonances in more than
one breast.

◪

VI *Ultima Ratio Regum*
◪

At sunset the following Sunday, Henri Christophe
had the feeling that his knees and his arms, though
still numb, might respond to a great enough effort
of the will. Turning himself clumsily over in bed,
he got his feet over the side, lying back as though
paralyzed from the waist up. His valet, Soliman,
helped him to stand. The King was then able to
walk slowly to the window like a big mechanical
toy. The Queen and the Princesses, notified by
the servant, came quietly into the room, stopping
beneath an equestrian statue of his Majesty. They
knew that there was too much drinking going on
in Haut-le-Cap. On the street-corners soup and
smoked meat were being served from huge kettles
by sweating cooks pounding the tables with skim-
mers and ladles. Between rows of laughing, shouting spectators, handkerchiefs fluttered in a dance.

The King drew in deep breaths of the afternoon air, and the oppressions that had weighed down his breast began to lift. Night was creeping down from the slopes of the mountains, blurring the outlines of trees and mazes. All at once Henri Christophe noticed that the musicians of the royal chamber were crossing the entrance court, carrying their instruments. Each displayed his professional deformity. The harpist stooped, as though humpbacked under the weight of his harp; another, thin as a rail, seemed pregnant with the drum that hung around his neck; another clasped a helicon. And bringing up the rear was a dwarf, almost hidden beneath a *pavillon chinois* that jingled at every step. The King's amazement that his musicians should be going off at such a time as though to give a concert at the foot of some solitary ceiba was interrupted by the ruffle of eight military drums. It was the hour of the changing of the guard. His Majesty took careful note of his grenadiers to make sure that during his illness the rigid discipline in which he had trained them had not been relaxed. But suddenly the monarch's hand rose in angry surprise. The untuned drums were not playing the prescribed call, but a syncopated tone in three beats produced not by the drumsticks, but by hands against the leather.

"They are playing the *mandoucouman*," Henri Christophe screamed, throwing his bicorne to the floor.

At that moment the guard broke ranks, crossing the esplanade in complete disorder. The officers were running with drawn swords. From the barracks windows clusters of men began to drop, coats open and pants drawn on over their boots. Shots were fired in the air. A color ensign slashed the flag of crowns and dolphins of the Prince's regiment. In the midst of the confusion a squad of light horsemen galloped away from the Palace at full speed, followed by the mules of a transport wagon loaded with saddles and harness. It was a general rout of uniforms to the sound of military drums beaten by fists. A malarial soldier, surprised by the mutiny, came out of the infirmary wrapped in a sheet, fastening the chin-strap of his shako. As he passed beneath the window where Henri Christophe stood, he made an obscene gesture and then ran off as fast as he could go. Then came the hush of evening, broken by the distant cry of a peacock. The King turned his head. In the night of the room Queen Marie-Louise and the Princesses Athenaïs and Améthyste were crying. Now it was clear why the people had been drinking so much that day in Haut-le-Cap.

Henri Christophe made his way through the Palace, supporting himself by banisters, curtains, and the backs of chairs. The absence of courtiers, flunkies, and guards made an oppressive emptiness of corridors and rooms. The walls seemed higher, the tiles broader. The Hall of Mirrors reflected only the figure of the King to the farthest reach of the most remote mirrors. And then, those buzzes, those slitherings, those crickets in the beamed ceilings which had never been heard before, and which now, with their intervals and rests, gave the silence a gamut of depth. The candles were slowly melting in the candelabra. A moth was circling the council room. After hurling itself against a gilded frame, an insect fell to the floor, first here, then there, with the unmistakable whirring of a flying beetle. The great reception room, with its two walls of windows, gave back the echo of Henri Christophe's heels, heightening his sense of utter loneliness. He descended by a service door to the kitchens where the fire was guttering out under the spits bare of meat. On the floor beside the carving table several empty wine bottles stood. The ropes of garlic hanging from the chimney lintel, the strings of dion-dion mushrooms, the smoked hams had all been carried away. The Palace was deserted, abandoned to the moonless night. It was the spoils of anyone who wanted to take it, for even the hunting dogs were gone. Henri Christophe returned to his floor. The white stairway rose sinisterly chill and lugubrious under the light of the candelabra. A bat that had come in through the skylight of the rotunda was flying in clumsy circles beneath the dull gold of the ceiling. The King leaned against the balustrade, seeking the solidity of the marble.

From below, where they sat on the bottom step of the stairway of honor, five young Negroes turned their troubled faces toward him. At that moment Henri Christophe felt a surge of love for them. They were the Royal Bonbons, Délivrance, Valentin, La Couronne, John, and Bien-Aimé, Africans whom the King had bought from a slave-trader to give them their freedom and have them trained as pages. Henri Christophe had always held himself aloof from the African mystique of the early leaders of Haitian independence, endeavoring to give his court a thoroughly European air. But now that he found himself alone, betrayed by his dukes, barons, generals, and ministers, the only ones who had remained faithful to him were those five Africans, those five youths of Congo, Fulah, or Mandingue origin, waiting like faithful dogs, their buttocks against the chill marble of the stairway, his *Ultima Ratio Regum*, which could no longer be issued from the cannon's mouth. Henri Christophe paused to look at them, made them an affectionate gesture, which they answered with a sorrowful bow, and then passed into the Throne Room.

He stopped before the canopy adorned with his coat of arms. Two crowned lions upheld a shield displaying a crowned phoenix, with a device reading *I rise from my ashes*. A pennant bore the motto of the flags, *God, my cause and my sword*. Henri Christophe opened a heavy coffer hidden under the fringes of the velvet. He took out a handful of silver coins stamped with his initials. Then he threw on the floor, one after the other, several solid-gold crowns of different weight. One of them rolled to the door and went thudding down the stairway with a noise that reverberated through the Palace. The King mounted his throne, his eyes on the yellow guttering candles on a candelabrum. Mechanically he recited the opening words of all the pronouncements of his government: "Henri, by the Grace of God and the Constitutional Law of the State, King of Haiti, Ruler of the Islands of La Tortue and Gonave, and others adjacent, Destroyer of Tyranny, Regenerator and Benefactor of the Haitian Nation, Creator of its Moral, Political, and Military Institutions, First Crowned Monarch of the New World, Defender of the Faith, Founder of the Royal and Military Order of Saint Henry, to all those present and to come, Greetings. . . ." Suddenly there came to Henri Christophe's mind the Citadel La Ferrière, his fortress up there above the clouds.

But at that moment the night grew dense with drums. Calling to one another, answering from mountain to mountain, rising from the beaches, issuing from the caves, running beneath the trees, descending ravines and riverbeds, the drums boomed, the *radas*, the *congos*, the drums of Bouckman, the drums of the Grand Alliances, all the drums of Voodoo. A vast encompassing percussion was advancing on Sans Souci, tightening the circle. A horizon of thunder closing in. A storm whose eye at the moment was the throne without heralds or mace-bearers. The King returned to his chamber and his window. The burning of his plantations had begun, of his dairies, of his canefields. Now the fire outran the drums, leaping from house to house, from field to field. A flame shot up from the granary, scattering red-black embers into the hay barn. The north wind lifted the burning husks of the cornfields, bringing them nearer and nearer. Fiery ash was falling on the Palace terraces.

Henri Christophe's thoughts went back to the Citadel. *Ultima Ratio Regum.* But that stronghold, unique in the world, was too vast for one man, and the monarch had never thought the day might come when he would find himself alone. The bulls' blood that those thick walls had drunk was an infallible charm against the arms of the white men. But this blood had never been directed against Negroes, whose shouts, coming closer now, were invoking Powers to which they made blood sacrifice. Henri Christophe, the reformer, had attempted to ignore Voodoo, molding with whiplash a caste of Catholic gentlemen. Now he realized that the

real traitors to his cause that night were St. Peter
with his keys, the Capuchins of St. Francis, the
blackamoor St. Benedict along with the dark-faced
Virgin in her blue cloak, and the Evangelists whose
books he had ordered kissed each time the oath of
loyalty was sworn. And, finally, all the martyrs,
those to whom he had ordered the lighting of
candles containing thirteen gold coins. After ful-
minating the white cupola of the chapel with a
glance of wrath, the chapel filled with images that
had turned their backs on him, symbols which had
gone over to the enemy, the King called for a
change of clothing and perfumes. He made the
Princesses leave the room, and dressed himself in
his richest ceremonial attire. He put on his broad
two-toned sash, the emblem of his investiture, tying
it above his sword hilt. The drums were now so
close that they seemed to be throbbing there, behind the balustrades of the main entrance, at the
foot of the great stone stairway. At that moment
the fire lighted up the mirrors of the Palace, the
crystal goblets, the crystal of the lamps, glasses,
windows, the mother-of-pearl inlay of the console
tables—the flames were everywhere, and it was
impossible to tell which were flames and which

reflections. All the mirrors of Sans Souci were simultaneously ablaze. The whole building disappeared under this chill fire, which reached out into the night, making each wall a cistern of twisted flames.

The shot was almost inaudible because of the proximity of the drums. Henri Christophe's hand released the pistol, to touch his gaping temple. His body stood erect for a moment, as though about to take a step, before it fell face forward amid all its decorations. The pages appeared on the threshold of the room. The King was dying, sprawled in his own blood.

🌿

VII   *Strait Is the Gate*
🌿

The African pages came out by a back door that faced the mountain, running as fast as they could, carrying on their shoulders a machete-trimmed branch from which hung a hammock through whose broken mesh the monarch's spurs emerged. Behind them, looking backward, stumbling in the darkness over the roots of the royal poinciana trees, came the Princesses Athenaïs and Améthyste, who had changed their shoes for the chambermaids' sandals, and the Queen, who had discarded her slippers when the stones of the road wrenched off a heel. Soliman, the King's valet, who had once been Pauline Bonaparte's masseur, brought up the rear, with a gun slung from a bandolier and a machete in his hand. As they plunged deeper into the tree-dense night of the mountains, the fire below could be seen thicker, more compact with flames, although it was beginning to die down as it reached the edges of the Palace esplanade. In the direction of Milot, however, the haymows had caught fire. Distant neighs, which sounded like the screams of tortured children, could be heard, as whole sides of the stables collapsed in a burst of fiery splinters, letting through a maddened horse with its mane singed and tail burned to the bone. Suddenly lights began to move in the Palace. It was a torch dance winding from kitchen to attics, entering by the open windows, ascending the stairways, running along the gutters, as though myriad glow-worms had taken possession of the upper floors. The looting had begun. The pages hurried on, knowing that this would entertain the rebels for a good time. Soliman put the safety on his rifle, slipping the butt of the gunstock under his arm.

By daybreak the fugitives had reached the outskirts of the Citadel La Ferrière. Their progress was slowed down because of the steepness of the ascent and the numerous cannon lying across the path, cannon that had never been mounted on their carriages, and would now lie there until they scaled away in rust. The sea was growing light in the direction of the Île de la Tortue as the chains of the drawbridge creaked sinisterly against the stone. Slowly the nail-studded doors of the Single Gate opened. And the corpse of Henri Christophe entered his Escorial boots first, wrapped in the hammock on which it had been borne by the Negro pages. Heavier with each step, it began to mount the inner stairways bedewed by the chilly drops that fell from the vaulted ceilings. Reveille calls shattered the dawn, answering one another from every corner of the fortress. Completely covered with red fungi, still filled with night, the Citadel emerged—blood-colored above, rust-colored below—out of the gray clouds swollen by the fires of the Plaine.

Now, in the middle of the Place d'Armes, the

E

fugitives related their tragic misfortune to the Governor of the fortress. Soon the news had spread through air-vents, tunnels, and corridors to the sleeping-quarters and kitchens. From every side soldiers began to appear, pushed forward by new uniforms coming down the stairways, leaving their batteries, descending from the watchtowers, deserting their posts. A cry of jubilation went up in the patio of the main tower, where the prisoners, released by their jailers, rushed from their cells, running with defiant rejoicing toward the members of the royal family. Hemmed in closer and closer by this mob, the disheveled pages, the shoeless Queen, the Princesses timidly guarded from insolent hands by Soliman, fell back toward a pile of fresh-mixed mortar intended for yet unfinished works, in which several shovels left by the masons still stood. Seeing that the situation was threatening to get out of hand, the Governor ordered the courtyard cleared. His order aroused a vast derisive laugh. One of the prisoners, so ragged that his genitals hung out of his pants, pointed a finger at the Queen's neck:

"In the whites' country, when a chief is killed, they cut off his wife's head."

As the Governor realized that the example set almost thirty years earlier by the idealists of the French Revolution was still vividly recalled by his men, it seemed to him that all was lost. But at that very moment a rumor that the company of the guard had decamped, hurrying down the hillside, suddenly gave a new turn to events. Running, falling over one another, by stairways and tunnels, the men made pell-mell for the Great Gate of the Citadel. Leaping, sliding, slipping, they dashed for the pathways, looking for shortcuts that would take them to Sans Souci as fast as possible. Henri Christophe's army was breaking up in a landslide. For the first time that huge edifice stood empty, taking on, with the vast silence of its rooms, the funereal solemnity of a royal tomb.

The Governor opened the hammock for a last look at his Majesty's countenance. With a knife he cut off one of the little fingers, handing it to the Queen, who slipped it into her boson, feeling it slide toward her stomach with the chill writhing of a worm. Then he gave an order, and the pages laid the body on the pile of mortar into which it slowly began to sink, as though pulled down by slimy hands. The corpse had curved a little as it was carried, still warm, up the mountainside. For that reason, the abdomen and thighs were the first to disappear. Arms and boots floated for a time, as though undecided, on the heaving gray surface of the mixture. Then all that remained was the face, held up by the frame of the bicorne clamped down from ear to ear. Lest the mortar should set before completely engulfing the head, the Governor laid his hand on the King's brow to push it down more quickly, with the gesture of one who takes a sick person's temperature. The mortar finally closed over the eyes of Henri Christophe, who now continued his slow descent into the entrails of a moisture that was growing less plastic. Then the corpse came to rest, one with the stone that imprisoned it.

Having chosen his own death, Henri Christophe would never know the corruption of his flesh, flesh fused with the very stuff of the fortress, inscribed in its architecture, integrated with its body bristling with flying buttresses. Le Bonnet de l'Évêque, the whole mountain, had become the mausoleum of the first King of Haiti.

Part Four

*I had fear of these visions
But since seeing these others,
My fear is grown greater.*

— *Calderón*

With a tinkling of bracelets and charms, Mlle
Athenaïs was accompanying on the newly acquired pianoforte her sister Améthyste, whose
slightly acid voice was embellishing with languid
portamenti an aria from Rossini's *Tancredi*. Wearing a white morning robe, a kerchief knotted about
her head in Haitian fashion, Queen Marie-Louise
sat embroidering an altar cloth intended for the
Capuchins of Pisa and scolding a cat that was
playing with her skeins of thread. After the tragic
days of the execution of the Dauphin Victor, after
their departure from Port-au-Prince with the help
of English merchants who had been purveyors to
the royal family, the Princesses, in Europe for the
first time, were enjoying a summer that seemed like
summer. Rome lived with doors open wide beneath a sun that made all the marbles shine, dis-
pelled the stench of the monks, and evoked the
calls of the orgeat-vendors. The city's thousand
bells tinkled with unaccustomed laziness beneath a
cloud-free sky that recalled the sky of the Plaine
in January. At last, sweaty, happy, warm again,

Athenaïs and Améthyste spent their days bare-
foot on the stone floors, their skirts unfastened,
tossing dice on the gameboard as they played at
royal goose, making lemonade, and pulling off the
shelves the latest novels, whose covers, after the
new fashion, were adorned with woodcuts of cemeteries at midnight, Scottish lakes, sylphs encircling
a young huntsman, maidens hiding a love letter in
the hollow of an old oak.

Soliman, too, found that Roman summer to his
liking. His appearance in the streets of the low
quarters—damp with dripping wash, dirty with
cabbage leaves, garbage, and coffee grounds—produced a veritable commotion. The shock brought
open the eyes of the blindest lazzaroni, the better
to see the Negro, while mandolin and hand-organ
fell mute. Some of the beggars thrust forward
stumps of arms, all their gamut of wounds and
mutilations, on the chance that this might be some
ambassador from across the sea. The children followed him wherever he went, organizing serenades
of harmonicas and jews'-harps. He was offered
glasses of wine in the taverns. As he passed, trades-
men came out of their shops to offer him a tomato
or a handful of nuts. Not for a long time had the

profile of a real Negro been silhouetted against a wall of Flaminio Ponzio or a door of Antonio Labacco. And he was asked to tell his life story, which he did with gusto, embellishing it with the greatest lies, passing himself off as a nephew of Henri Christophe who had miraculously escaped the slaughter of the Cap the night when the death squad had had to finish off one of the King's natural sons with bayonets because several volleys had failed to bring him down. His gaping audience had no clear idea of where all these things had taken place. Some thought it was Madagascar, others Persia or the land of the Berbers. There was always someone eager to wipe his face with a handkerchief, when he began to sweat, to see if the color came off. One afternoon, as a joke, they took him to one of the narrow, foul-smelling theaters where *opere buffe* were sung. After the finale of a plot that had to do with Italians in Algiers, he was pushed onto the stage. His unexpected appearance was such a hit with the spectators that the manager of the company invited him to repeat the performance whenever he liked. Now, to make things even better, he was having a love affair with one of the maids at the Borghese Palace, a sturdy Piedmontese

E*

girl who had no taste for sugar-candy lovers. On the really hot days Soliman was in the habit of taking long siestas in the grass of the Forum, where flocks of sheep were always pastured. The ruins threw a pleasant shade over the abundant grass, and if one dug in the dirt a little it was not unusual to find a marble ear, a stone ornament, or an oxidized coin. The spot was sometimes chosen by a streetwalker to ply her trade with a seminary student. But its most assiduous visitors were persons of a thoughtful turn of mind, priests carrying green umbrellas, Englishmen with delicate hands who went into raptures at the sight of a broken column, copying down some half-effaced inscription. Toward evening the Negro would go into the Borghese Palace by the service entrance and give himself over to uncorking bottles of red wine in the company of the girl from the Piedmont. Complete disorder reigned in the mansion, for the owners were away. The lamps at the door were dark with fly-specks, the servants' liveries were filthy, the coachmen were drunk all the time, the carriage was unpolished, and the cobwebs in the library were so thick that for years nobody had wanted to enter it for fear that disgusting insects would crawl

down the neck or even into the bosom. If it had not
been that a young abbot, a nephew of the Prince,
lived in one of the upper apartments, the servants
would have moved upstairs to sleep in the beds
formerly occupied by cardinals.

Late one night, when Soliman and his light-of-
love were alone in the kitchen, the Negro, completely drunk, decided to explore beyond the servants' quarters. Following a long corridor, the two
of them came out into an immense patio filled with
marbles shimmering in the moonlight. Two rows
of superimposed columns framed the patio, casting
the outline of their capitals halfway up the wall.
Raising and lowering the street lantern she carried,
the Piedmontese girl revealed to Soliman the array
of statues that filled one of the lateral galleries.
They were all of naked women, although all wore
veils that an imaginary breeze coyly swept across
such spots as decency demanded. There were many
animals, too, for one of the ladies held a swan in
her arms, another was clasping the neck of a bull,
others were running with hounds or fleeing from
horned men with goat-legs who were probably related to the devil. It was a white, cold, motionless
world, but its shadows took on life and grew under

the light of the lantern, as though those beings with unseeing eyes, who looked without looking, were moving about their midnight visitors. With that gift of the drunk for seeing horrible things out of the tail of the eye, Soliman thought that one of the statues had lowered its arms a little. Uneasily he pulled the Piedmontese girl toward a stairway leading to the upper rooms. Now paintings seemed to step from the wall: a smiling youth who raised a curtain, a boy, crowned with grape leaves, who held a mute panpipe to his lips or laid a finger to his mouth for silence. After crossing a gallery adorned with mirrors painted with flowers, the chambermaid, with a provocative gesture, opened a small walnut door and lowered the lantern.

Against the farther wall of that small chamber a single statue stood. It was a naked woman lying on a bed and holding out an apple. Trying to collect his disordered thoughts, Soliman made his stumbling way toward the statue. Surprise had sobered him a little. He knew that face, and the body, too; that whole body aroused a memory. He touched the marble with eager hands, his sense of smell and sight in his fingers. He felt the breasts. He ran a curved palm over the belly, letting his little finger rest in the depression of the navel. He caressed the tender hollow of the back, as though to turn the body over. His fingers sought the rounded hips, the delicate thigh, the terseness of the breast. That voyage of his fingers refreshed his memory, bringing back distant images. He had known this contact before. With this same circular movement he had one day relieved the pain of a twisted ankle. The substance was different, but the forms were the same. Now those nights of fear on the Île de la Tortue came back to him, when a French general had lain dying behind a closed door. He recalled her whose head he had stroked to put her to sleep. And, suddenly, moved by a memory not to be gainsaid, Soliman began to go through the motions of a masseur, following the structure of the muscles, the outline of the tendons, rubbing the back from the middle outward, stroking the breast muscles, tapping with his forefinger here and there. But suddenly the chill of the marble rising to his wrists as with pincers of death stiffened him into a cry. The wine in his head began to whirl. This statue, yellow in the light of the lantern, was the corpse of Pauline Bonaparte, a corpse newly stiffened, recently stripped of breath and sight, which perhaps there was still time to bring back to life. With a terrible cry, as though his breast were riven, the Negro began to shout, shout as loud as he could, in the vast silence of the Borghese Palace. And his look became so primitive, his heels stamped so strongly on the floor, turning the chapel beneath into a drumhead, that the horrified Piedmontese fled down the stairs, leaving Soliman alone with the *Venus* of Canova.

The courtyard came ablaze with candles and lanterns. Awakened by the voice that had reverberated so powerfully from the second floor, the footmen and coachmen emerged from their rooms in shirtsleeves, pulling up their pants. There was a loud banging of the knocker at the side door, which was opened to let in the gendarmes of the night patrol, who filed in followed by several frightened neighbors. As the mirrors were lighted up, the Negro turned sharply about. Those lights, the people crowding into the patio among the white marble statues, the unmistakable bicornes, the uniforms with their light piping, the cold curve of an unsheathed sword brought back to him in a second's shiver the night of Henri Christophe's death. Swinging a chair through a window, Soliman leaped to the street. And the first matins found him shivering with fever—for he had fallen victim to the malaria of the Pontine Marshes—and calling on Papa Legba to carry him back to Santo Domingo. His hands still felt the excruciating touch of nightmare. It seemed to him that he had fallen into a trance upon the stones of a grave, as happened Back There to certain of the possessed, whom the peasants both feared and revered because they were on better terms than anyone else with the Masters of the Graveyards.

In vain did Queen Marie-Louise attempt to calm him with an infusion of bitter herbs which she had received from the Cap, via London, as a special token from President Boyer. Soliman was cold. An unseasonable fog was chilling the marbles of Rome. The summer was veiled by a mist that thickened by the hour. The Princesses sent for Dr. Antommarchi, who had been Napoleon's doctor on St. Helena, and who was credited by some with exceptional professional gifts, particularly as a homeopath. But the pills he prescribed never left the box. Turning his back on all, moaning to the wall papered with yellow flowers on a green background, Soliman was seeking a god who had his abode in far-off Dahomey, at some dark crossroad, his red phallus on a crutch he carried for that purpose.

Papa Legba, l'ouvri barrié-a pou moin, agó yé,
Papa Legba, ouvri barrié-a pou moin, pou
moin passé.

🌿

II   *The Royal Palace*
🌿

Ti Noël had been among the ringleaders in the sack of the Palace of Sans Souci. As a result, the ruins of the old manor house of Lenormand de Mézy were bizarrely furnished. The building continued roofless for lack of two points of support on which to rest a beam or rooftree. But with his machete the old man had pried away fallen stones, bringing to light parts of the foundation, a windowsill, three steps, a piece of a wall that still displayed, clinging to the brick, the molding of the old Norman dining-room. The night the Plaine teemed with men, women, and children carrying on their heads pendulum clocks, chairs, draperies, saints' canopies, girandoles, prayer stools, lamps, and washbasins, Ti Noël had made several trips to Sans Souci. In this way he had become the owner of a *boule* table that stood before the straw-strewn fireplace where he slept, hidden from sight behind a Coromandel screen covered with dim figures against a dull-gold background. An embalmed moonfish, the gift of the Royal Society of London to Prince Victor, lay on the tiles of a floor pushed up by grass and roots alongside a music box and a decanter whose thick green glass held bubbles the color of the rainbow. He had also carried off a doll dressed as a shepherdess, an armchair upholstered in tapestry, and three volumes of the *Grande Encyclopédie* on which he was in the habit of sitting to eat sugar cane.

But the pride of the old man's heart was a dress coat that had belonged to Henri Christophe, of green silk, with cuffs of salmon-colored lace, which he wore all the time, his regal air heightened by a braided straw hat that he had folded and crushed into the shape of a bicorne, adding a red flower in lieu of a cockade. Of an afternoon he could be seen sitting among his weather-exposed furniture playing with the doll, which opened and closed its eyes, or winding his music box, which repeated from sunrise to sunset the same German Ländler. Ti Noël now talked continually. He talked, his arms opened wide, in the middle of the roads; he talked to the washerwomen kneeling beside the sandy brooks with their breasts bare; he talked to the children dancing in a circle. But most of all he talked when he sat behind his table, holding a guava twig in his hand as a scepter. To his mind came blurred recollections of things told by Macandal, the One-Armed, so many years back that he could not recall when. In those days he began to have the conviction that he had a mission to carry out, although no intimation, no sign, had revealed its nature to him. However, it was something great, something commensurate with the rights acquired by one whose days had been so long on the earth, forgotten by his children concerned only with their own children, on this and the other side of the sea. Moreover, it was clear that great things were about to take place. When the women saw him approaching, they waved bright cloths in sign of reverence, like the palms spread before Jesus one Sunday. When he passed a cabin, the old women invited him to sit down, bringing him a little raw rum in a gourd or a newly rolled cigar. At a festival of drums, Ti Noël had been possessed by the spirit of the King of Angola, and had pronounced a long speech filled with riddles and promises. Then herds had appeared on his lands. Those new animals that grazed among the ruins were undoubtedly gifts from his subjects. Seated in his armchair, his coat unbuttoned, his straw hat pulled down to his ears, slowly scratching his bare belly, Ti Noël issued orders to the wind. But they were the edicts of a peaceable government, inasmuch as no tyranny of whites or Negroes seemed to offer a threat to his liberty. The old man filled the gaps in the tumbledown walls with fine things, appointed any passer-by a minister, any hay-gatherer a general, distributing baronetcies, presenting wreaths, blessing the little girls, and awarding flowers for services rendered. It was thus the Order of the Bitter Broom had come into being, the Order of the Christmas Gift, the Order of the Pacific Ocean, and the Order of the Nightshade. But the most sought after was the Order of the Sunflower, which was the most decorative. As the half of a tiled floor which constituted his Audience Chamber was very good for dancing, his palace would fill up with countryfolk, who brought their reed pipes, their *cháchás*, and their drums. Lighted faggots were fitted into forked branches and Ti Noël, more majestic than ever in his green coat, presided over the feast, seated between a priest of the Savanna, who represented the native church that had sprung up, and an old veteran, one of those who had fought against Rochambeau at Vertières, who brought out for special occasions his campaign uniform of faded blue and red that had turned strawberry from the rain that leaked into his house.

¥

III *The Surveyors*
¥

But one morning the Surveyors appeared. One had to have seen the Surveyors at work to grasp the terror aroused by the presence of these beings who pursue the calling of insects. The Surveyors who had come down to the Plaine from distant Port-au-Prince beyond the cloudy hills were silent, light-skinned men wearing—it must be admitted—fairly normal attire, who stretched long cords along the ground, drove stakes, carried plummets,

looked through telescopes, and bristled with measuring rods and squares. When Ti Noël saw these
suspicious characters going and coming on his domain, he spoke severely to them. But the Surveyors
paid no attention to him. They went here and there
insolently, measuring everything and writing
things in their gray books with thick carpenter's
pencils. The old man observed with rage that they
spoke the language of the French, that language
which he had forgotten since the days when
M. Lenormand de Mézy had bet and lost him in a
card game in Santiago de Cuba. Ti Noël ordered
the sons-of-bitches off his land, shouting so furi-
ously that one of the Surveyors grabbed him by
the back of the neck, and to remove him from the
field of vision of his telescope gave him a sound
whack across the belly with his measuring stick.
The old man withdrew to his chimney, peering out
from behind the Coromandel screen to growl mal-
edictions. But the next day, roaming the Plaine in
search of something to eat, he noted that there
were Surveyors everywhere, and that mounted
mulattoes, wearing shirts open at the throat, silk
sashes, and military boots, were directing vast
operations of plowing and clearing carried out by

hundreds of Negro prisoners. Astride their donkeys, carrying the hens and pigs, hundreds of peasants were leaving their cabins amid the weeping and lamentation of the women, to seek refuge in the hills. Ti Noël learned from a fugitive that farm work had been made obligatory, and that the whip was now in the hands of Republican mulattoes, the new masters of the Plaine du Nord.

Macandal had not foreseen this matter of forced labor. Nor had Bouckman, the Jamaican. The ascendancy of the mulattoes was something new that had not occurred to José Antonio Aponte, beheaded by the Marquis of Someruelos, whose record of rebellion Ti Noël had learned of during his slave days in Cuba. Not even Henri Christophe would have suspected that the land of Santo Domingo would bring forth this spurious aristocracy, this caste of quadroons, which was now taking over the old plantations, with their privileges and rank. The old man raised his beclouded eyes to the Citadel La Ferrière. But his gaze could no longer travel so far. The word of Henri Christophe had become stone and no longer dwelt among us. All of his fabulous person that remained was in Rome, a finger floating in a rock-crystal bottle filled with brandy. And in keeping with that example, Queen Marie-Louise, after taking her daughters to the baths of Carlsbad, had ordered in her will that her right foot be preserved in alcohol and given to the Capuchins of Pisa to be kept in a chapel built by her pious munificence. Try as he would, Ti Noël could think of no way to help his subjects bowed once again beneath the whiplash. The old man began to lose heart at this endless return of chains, this rebirth of shackles, this proliferation of suffering, which the more resigned began to accept as proof of the uselessness of all revolt. Ti Noël was afraid that he, too, would be ordered to the furrow in spite of his age, and as a result the thought of Macandal took hold of his memory. Inasmuch as human guise brought with it so many calamities, it would be better to lay it aside for a time, and observe events on the Plaine in some less conspicuous form. Once he had come to this decision, Ti Noël was astonished at how easy it is to turn into an animal when one has the necessary powers. In proof of this he climbed a tree, willed himself to become a bird, and instantly was a bird. He watched the Surveyors from the top of a branch, digging his beak into the violated flesh of a medlar. The next day he willed himself to be a stallion, and he was a stallion, but he had to run off as fast as he could from a mulatto who tried to lasso him and geld him with a kitchen knife. He turned himself into a wasp, but he soon tired of the monotonous geometry of wax constructions. He made the mistake of becoming an ant, only to find himself carrying heavy loads over interminable paths under the vigilance of big-headed ants who reminded him unpleasantly of Lenormand de Mézy's overseers, Henri Christophe's guards, and the mulattoes of today. At times a horse's hooves destroyed a column of workers, killing hundreds of them. When this happened, the big-headed ants straightened out the file again, retraced the path, and all went on as before, in the same busy coming and going. As Ti Noël was there in disguise, and did not for a moment consider himself one of the species, he took refuge by himself under his table, which that night was his shelter against a steady drizzle that filled the fields with the hay-like odor of wet rushes.

🕮

IV *Agnus Dei*
🕮

It was going to be a hot, overcast day. The dew had no more than dried from the cobwebs when a great noise descended from the sky upon the lands of Ti Noël. Running and stumbling as they dropped came the geese from the old barnyards of Sans Souci, the geese that had escaped the sack because the Negroes do not like their meat, and that had lived as they pleased, all this time, among the canebrakes of the hills. The old man received them with great rejoicing, happy over their visit, for there were not many who knew, as he did, the intelligence and cheerfulness of geese, for he had taken notice of their model habits when M. Lenormand de Mézy had attempted years before, without much success, to acclimate them. As they were not made for a hot climate, the females laid only five eggs every two years. But this clutch gave rise to a series of rites whose ceremonies were handed down from generation to generation. On the bank of a shallow stream the nuptials took place in the presence of the entire clan of geese and ganders.

A young male took his mate for life, covering her amid a chorus of jubilant honkings accompanied by a ritual dance consisting of turns, stamping, and arabesques of the neck. Then the whole clan set about building the nest. During the incubation period the bride was watched over by the males, on the alert all night even though their round eyes were tucked under a wing. When some danger threatened the clumsy, canary-downed goslings, the oldest gander directed charges of breast and beak, heedless of whether the adversary was mastiff, horseman, or carriage. Geese were orderly beings, with principles and systems, whose existence denied all superiority of individual over individual of the same species. The principle of authority represented by the Oldest Gander was a measure whose object was to maintain order within the clan, after the manner of the king or head of the old African assemblies. Ti Noël employed his magic powers to transform himself into a goose and live with the fowl that had made his domain their abode.

But, when he attempted to take his place in the clan, he encountered sawtoothed beaks and outstretched necks that kept him at a distance. He was made to keep to the edge of the pasture, and the indifferent females were surrounded by a wall of white feathers. In view of this Ti Noël tried to be circumspect, and not draw too much attention to himself, to approve the decisions of the others. His reward was contempt and a shrugging of wings. In vain did he reveal to the females where certain succulent watercress was to be found. Their gray tails twitched with displeasure and their yellow eyes regarded him with haughty suspicion, repeated by the eyes on the other side of the head. The clan now seemed a community of aristocrats, tightly closed against anyone of a different caste. The Great Gander of Sans Souci would have refused to have anything to do with the Great Gander of Dondon. Had they met face to face, hostilities would have ensued. Thus Ti Noël quickly gathered that even if he persisted in his efforts for years, he would never be admitted in any capacity to the rites and duties of the clan. It had been made crystal clear to him that being a goose did not imply that all geese were equal. No known goose had sung or danced the day of Ti Noël's wedding. None of those alive had seen him hatch out. He presented himself, without proper family back-

ground, before geese who could trace their ances-
try back four generations. In a word, he was an
upstart, an intruder.

Ti Noël vaguely understood that his rejection
by the geese was a punishment for his cowardice.
Macandal had disguised himself as an animal for
years to serve men, not to abjure the world of
men. It was then that the old man, resuming his
human form, had a supremely lucid moment. He
lived, for the space of a heartbeat, the finest moments of his life; he glimpsed once more the heroes
who had revealed to him the power and the full-
ness of his remote African forebears, making him
believe in the possible germinations the future held.
He felt countless centuries old. A cosmic weari-
ness, as of a planet weighted with stones, fell upon
his shoulders shrunk by so many blows, sweats,
revolts. Ti Noël had squandered his birthright,
and, despite the abject poverty to which he had
sunk, he was leaving the same inheritance he had
received: a body of flesh to which things had happened. Now he understood that a man never
knows for whom he suffers and hopes. He suffers
and hopes and toils for people he will never know,
and who, in turn, will suffer and hope and toil for

others who will not be happy either, for man always seeks a happiness far beyond that which is meted out to him. But man's greatness consists in the very fact of wanting to be better than he is. In laying duties upon himself. In the Kingdom of Heaven there is no grandeur to be won, inasmuch as there all is an established hierarchy, the unknown is revealed, existence is infinite, there is no possibility of sacrifice, all is rest and joy. For this reason, bowed down by suffering and duties, beautiful in the midst of his misery, capable of loving in the face of afflictions and trials, man finds his greatness, his fullest measure, only in the Kingdom of This World.

Ti Noël climbed upon his table, scuffing the marquetry with his calloused feet. Toward the Cap the sky was dark with the smoke of fires as on the night when all the conch shells of the hills and coast had sung together. The old man hurled his declaration of war against the new masters, ordering his subjects to march in battle array against the insolent works of the mulattoes in power. At that moment a great green wind, blowing from the ocean, swept the Plaine du Nord, spreading through the Dondon valley with a loud roar. And while the slaughtered bulls bellowed on the summit of Le Bonnet de l'Évêque, the armchair, the screen, the volumes of the *Encyclopédie*, the music box, the doll, and the moonfish rose in the air, as the last ruins of the plantation came tumbling down. The trees bowed low, tops southward, roots wrenched from the earth. And all night long the sea, turned to rain, left trails of salt on the flanks of the mountains.

From that moment Ti Noël was never seen again, nor his green coat with the salmon lace cuffs, except perhaps by that wet vulture who turns every death to his own benefit and who sat with outspread wings, drying himself in the sun, a cross of feathers which finally folded itself up and flew off into the thick shade of Bois Caïman.